WHISKEY UNDONE

A Whiskey and Lies Novel

CARRIE ANN RYAN

Whiskey Undone
A Whiskey and Lies Novel
By: Carrie Ann Ryan
© 2018 Carrie Ann Ryan
ISBN: 978-1-943123-92-6
Cover Art by Charity Hendry
Photograph ©2016 Jenn LeBlanc / Illustrated Romance

For more information, please join Carrie Ann Ryan's MAILING LIST. To interact with Carrie Ann Ryan, you can join her FAN CLUB

Praise for Carrie Ann Ryan....

"Carrie Ann Ryan knows how to pull your heartstrings and make your pulse pound! Her wonderful Redwood Pack series will draw you in and keep you reading long into the night. I can't wait to see what comes next with the new generation, the Talons. Keep them coming, Carrie Ann!" – Lara Adrian, New York Times bestselling author of CRAVE THE NIGHT

"Carrie Ann Ryan never fails to draw readers in with passion, raw sensuality, and characters that pop off the page. Any book by Carrie Ann is an absolute treat." – New York Times Bestselling Author J. Kenner

"With snarky humor, sizzling love scenes, and brilliant, imaginative worldbuilding, The Dante's Circle series reads as if Carrie Ann Ryan peeked at my personal wish list!" – NYT Bestselling Author, Larissa Ione

"Carrie Ann Ryan writes sexy shifters in a world full of

To my best friend.
I fell for you just like they did.
And I miss you more with each passing day.

Acknowledgments

I fell in love with Whiskey and it's all thanks to this series and the people who work with me on it. Every time I dive into Whiskey, Pennsylvania, I'm not alone and there are a lot of people to thank.

Thank you Chelle for not only being my rock, my touch stone, but for being a fantastic editor. And for holding my hand when I went a little too Criminal Minds all the while wanting me to go even darker.

Thank you Charity and Jenn for your work on this cover. This series makes me so happy!

Thank you Tara for listening to me when I send twenty emails in a day and yet answer each and every one of them.

Thank you Mom and Dad for being fantastic and holding me when I needed it. And thank you Mom for walking into your living room asking how many words I had down even though I was there to visit you and yet I was still on deadline.

Thank you Andi, Marni, Anne, and Maxine for your help and work on this book. I'm thrilled with what we've come up with and I love it!

Thank you dear readers for loving Whiskey and my books. Without you, I couldn't do this. While this is the final Whiskey book, it's not the final book in this world. So thank you for following me and reading.

And while I'm here, thank you Dan. I miss you and our kitten miss you too. Love you.

WHISKEY UNDONE

Two best friends follow a dangerous and seductive path in the final standalone novel of the bestselling Whiskey and Lies series from NYT Bestselling Author Carrie Ann Ryan.

Ainsley Harris has always kept a secret from her best friend. She's stood by his side, helped him raise his daughter, and tried to keep her distance even though she's been in love with him for years. She knows he has secrets of his own and she's not willing to chance what they have on a possibility.

Loch Collins has hidden himself and his past from the world for good reason. Darkness always comes back to haunt those who fight against it, and he knows better than most. One night of temper, however, forces him to realize his true feelings for Ainsley—for better or worse.

But Loch's former allies aren't on his side anymore,

and now not only is his life and the life of his daughter on the line, but Ainsley is in the crosshairs, as well. Together, two best friends must fight for each other and their small town, because Whiskey has never burned brighter. And danger, it seems, is ever lurking.

Chapter 1

*L*och Collins knew the night wasn't going to end anytime soon, but the pounding in his head wished it would. He'd been up most of the night dealing with paperwork and his daughter. Misty's nightmares had forced him to wake up earlier than usual to open his gym since his morning rotation crew had called in sick.

To say he was exhausted, irritated, and not in the mood to deal with people was an understatement. But even though he wanted to walk out of the bar and head to his bed for eight hours of uninterrupted sleep, he knew he would never be able to, not with his mother giving him looks over her shoulder as he casually crept to the other end of the bar nearest the door.

The woman seemed to have eyes in the back of her head, and ever since he was little, she had been able to figure out what he was doing before he even had a chance to attempt it. Today was the engagement and new baby celebration for his brother Fox and his fiancée Melody at Loch's other brother Dare's whiskey bar and restaurant. He knew there was another name for the event, but for the life of him, he couldn't think of it. They'd closed down this part of the bar for an hour just for family, and it would open up soon for the rest of the town and the tourists. Each of the family members had homes large enough for a party, but Dare's bar was a great place for them all to congregate and not have to drive after a few glasses of whiskey.

"Why are you sulking over in the corner while the rest of the family is smiling and drinking?"

Loch looked down at his best friend and raised a brow.

Ainsley just rolled her eyes and elbowed him in the gut. He didn't move, but he did have to hold back a wince. He'd taught her enough self-defense lessons over the years that those bony elbows of hers did real damage—not that he wanted her to know that he'd felt the impact.

"I'm not sulking." He folded his arms over his chest but didn't turn to her since he didn't want his family to notice that he wasn't really paying attention. He was usually better at family gatherings, but today just wasn't his day. Apparently, both his mother *and* Ainsley had noticed.

"You're sulking. And don't give me another eyebrow raise. You might have perfected that for everyone else, but I can always see through it. You don't intimidate me." Ainsley folded her arms right under her breasts and glared at him, though he saw the humor in those hazel eyes.

She'd let her hair down tonight, and the long, brown waves with honey-colored highlights flowed over her shoulders. Loch always liked it when she wore her hair down, but she didn't do it as often as he might like. Whether she had it up in a high ponytail or down like it was now, her hair always brought out the sharp features of her face. His mother had once said that Ainsley's cheekbones could cut glass, and he supposed he agreed with her. He glanced down at his best friend's lips and noticed she wore gloss today with no color, something she often did since she'd once told him that she didn't like how thin her lips were. When he'd said that he liked them just fine, she'd just rolled her eyes and huffed something about being a man and not knowing what good lips looked like. He hadn't responded, but he figured since he was the one looking at her, he should know what he liked in lips.

Not that he'd ever say that to Ainsley since talking about his best friend's lips or any other part of her body was definitely off-limits.

As it should be.

"You're staring at me. And still sulking. Perhaps even scowling. What is up with you tonight?"

"Nothing is up with me. Go bother Dare or Fox and leave me be." He hadn't meant to snap at her, but he was in a shitty mood, and thinking about Ainsley's lips hadn't helped matters.

"You're an idiot," she whispered under her breath.

"And an asshole. So, get your head out of your ass and go hug your brother. Because he's engaged and happy and he's allowed to be."

This time, Loch turned to her, frowning. "I'm not an asshole." *Yes, he was.* "And I never said Fox shouldn't be happy."

"You're sure acting like you think that. You're over here in the corner while your brother and his woman are celebrating a new baby and the fact that Melody will soon be family. Dare and Kenzie are celebrating too since they're also engaged. Everyone is happy and starting a new life. And you're glaring."

Loch didn't like the fact that she was calling him out but, frankly, he didn't know why he had to be here the whole night. This wasn't the real engagement party, that would come later. This was just a drink or two with the family while they talked about planning and other things that had nothing to do with him. He wasn't usually this anti-social, but hell, he'd had a long day, a longer week, and an even longer year, and all he wanted to do was sleep. It didn't help that he knew his daughter was at the babysitter's at the moment and would be spending the night with his parents for grandparent time. Therefore, the house would be empty for him to just rest in peace.

All he wanted was sleep, damn it.

"I'm only glaring at you right now, Ainsley. Get off my back and go join the family." He had no idea why the cutting words were slipping from his mouth like they were, but as soon as he said them, he knew he couldn't take them back.

For a moment, he thought he saw hurt in her eyes, but she quickly blinked it away as if it had never been there at all.

"Like I said. Asshole. What I don't get is why tonight, Loch? Why do you have to be an asshole tonight? I just don't understand you sometimes, and for being your so-called best friend, that's saying something." Ainsley stormed off for a moment before slowing her steps and brushing her hair over her shoulders so it fell down her back. He couldn't see her face, but he figured she'd put on a smile for Kenzie, Dare's fiancée, and Melody.

Both women gave Loch a look over the top of Ainsley's head, and he figured his best friend's smile hadn't been good enough to mask her true feelings.

Well, fuck. Turned out he *was* an asshole. But it wasn't like he'd denied it before. At least to himself.

While his parents talked to Kenzie, Melody, and Ainsley, his brothers walked over to him, whiskeys in hand, and a spare one in Dare's grip for Loch. Loch gladly took the glass from his brother and saluted them both before taking a sip. The whiskey his brother had chosen wasn't the one to knock back in one gulp but rather take in slowly. No matter how much Loch needed the jolt to his system, he took his time.

The three brothers looked alike, and even their little sister, Tabby, who lived out in Denver with her husband looked like them. They all had dark hair and blue eyes, features which had come from their father. There were subtle differences in each of their faces, and most of that came from their mother's side of the family. While Tabby was of average height and slender of build, the rest of the siblings were all a bit taller than average. Loch was not only the tallest and biggest of the bunch thanks to his career owning a gym and his other job he didn't much talk about, but he was also the eldest of the four.

And the only one who wasn't married, engaged, or thinking of having more children—not that he was complaining.

He already had his one perfect daughter. He didn't need any more. Nor did he need a serious relationship, or anything headed down that road. He'd thought he had that once with Misty's mother, but once the baby was born, Marnie, his ex, had signed over legal rights to Misty and hightailed it out of town, never once looking back.

Loch had found himself alone in his hometown of Whiskey, Pennsylvania, trying to figure out how to raise a little baby girl on his own. He hadn't exactly been alone, of course. His parents had stepped up, as did Fox and Dare when Dare moved back to Whiskey after leaving the police force. Tabby had already been living in Denver at that point, but she had made him countless lists and charts so he could find his way while figuring out how to be a parent.

And, of course, there was Ainsley.

She'd been his everything.

His babysitter. His friend. His protector from his darkest thoughts. His savior.

She'd been the person up late at night, pacing with him when Misty's cholic had kept her up for hours in pain and crying. She'd been the one helping him cook meals so he could work the hours he needed to. Though neither of them was the best of cooks, they'd made do. She'd stepped in when Loch hadn't been able to ask for help, and she hadn't requested a thing in return.

Honestly, she was more of a mother to Misty than Marnie ever was, and he'd never be able to find the words to tell her how truly thankful he was—even if he hated himself a bit more each day for relying on her as much as he did.

She was his everything, and yet...his nothing. Nothing more than she should be anyway.

Snapping back to the present, Loch saw his brothers giving him curious looks, and realized he'd been staring at Ainsley rather than talking to them. Who knew how long he'd been standing there looking like an idiot. And his headache certainly hadn't gotten any better in the time being.

"You going to keep glaring, or are you going to act like you're a Collins and get your ass in gear and celebrate?" Dare stared at him, and Loch flipped his brother off.

"Aw, family love right there," Fox drawled.

"I hate you both sometimes," Loch said quietly.

"We know," they said in unison.

"What's up with you, really?" Dare asked, leaning forward and lowering his voice.

Loch shook his head. "Nothing. Just didn't get enough sleep and, according to Ainsley, I'm an asshole."

"Well…she's not wrong," Fox added.

Loch flipped his other brother off before taking another sip of his whiskey. He let the smoky taste settle on his tongue before swallowing. Dare's bar had a variety of whiskeys like most bars around the world, but Loch preferred Dare's. The bar had been renovated a few times over the years from back when it was part of a small and illegal distillery during the era of Prohibition, but Loch figured Dare's twist on the historic bar and restaurant with its wide array of delicious spirits was by far the best.

Not that his judgement was biased or anything when it came to his family.

"You don't have to stay," Dare said quickly. "I mean, you showed up, we ate, and now you've had a drink. You can walk home and just be by yourself. No one is going to care."

"Mom and Ainsley will."

"If Mom knew you were tired and had a headache, she wouldn't." At Loch's look, Fox added quickly, "I know you have one because you keep touching your temple. Maybe drinking isn't the best thing for you right now. Whiskey doesn't always lead to the best decisions."

"Considering you're marrying the woman you had too much to drink with and are having a baby with her thanks to said whiskey, I don't know if you're the best person to comment on that. Seems to have worked out for you," Loch said dryly.

"True enough." Fox looked over his shoulder and smiled at Melody, who grinned right back. Loch was only just getting to know his future sister-in-law, but he liked her. Loch knew she'd been through hell and back—a few times —but she had come out stronger for it. Fox loved the woman, and anything or anyone that made his brother smile like that was perfect in his book.

He shook himself from his thoughts and focused on his brothers again. "I can't leave now without annoying Ainsley, and since I've been pissing her off more often than not recently, I don't plan to do it again."

"Good man." Dare snorted. "Now, come over here and finish off the cake with us then head home. You're tired, we get it. Don't overwork yourself trying to do it all."

"I don't." Another lie.

"Yeah, you do. We're all like that, but I'm pretty sure you do it the most." Fox sipped from his glass, meeting Loch's gaze.

"True enough. Let me get some cake, and then I'll head out. Sounds like a plan."

Dare gripped Loch's shoulder and gave it a squeeze before the three of them made their way over to the others. His mother did indeed give Loch a look, but he sidled up next to Ainsley and sipped his drink—just one since he already had a headache—and ate the cake Ainsley handed to him. Eventually, he had more fun than he thought he would and was glad his brothers had pulled him over. He loved his family, liked spending time with them, but he sometimes forgot not to live in his head, constantly dealing with his own problems.

By the time they parted ways, each of the siblings and their women going to their own houses, and Loch's parents off to pick up Dare's son and Misty for a slumber party, Loch was ready for bed.

"Mind if I go with you to your house?" Ainsley asked. "I know you're tired, but I left my laptop there earlier like an idiot, and I need it for tomorrow morning."

Loch took his best friend's hand and gave it a squeeze. He'd been a jerk all night and hated that he'd acted like he had. Ainsley froze and gave him a weird look but didn't react otherwise.

"Of course. You need me to drive you home after? Your car is at your house, right?" They waved at everyone as they left, but Loch kept his hand on hers, wanting to make sure she knew he was sorry for being an asshole.

"I can walk easily enough. It's not that late, and it's a decent night for a walk." Ainsley didn't move her hand from his, and he took it as a sign that she forgave him. Or she'd forgotten that she was holding his hand. Or was possibly chilled, since it *was* the end of winter in Pennsylvania.

"Then let's get out of the cold," Loch said quickly as they walked down the sidewalk, passing tourists and townsfolk, who were on their way to other places along the main road of Whiskey. A lot of the town's income came from tourism, and while the weather might not be *too* cold at the moment, it was still their downtime.

There was snow coming, Loch could feel it. Once it stopped and stayed on the trees surrounding the old buildings and landmarks, people would come in droves again to take photos and buy trinkets. Some would stay longer for a meal at his brother's place, maybe rent a room at the family inn Kenzie ran. Others would join a dance class at Melody's studio or stop by Loch's gym for a workout. They would read the paper with Fox's stories, and talk about what was going on in the world as they strolled Whiskey's streets. Those that lived locally would send their children to Ainsley's school. All of them were connected to the town in some way. Even if they tried to get away, Whiskey was a part of them.

"How goes school?" He pulled Ainsley close as someone bumped into her, and she leaned into him as they made their way to his house.

"Tiring, but worth it. I love my kids this year, even though I swear the grading is worse than ever. I'm looking forward to spring break, and we're only halfway there from winter break as it is."

He smiled down at her. "I did the same when I was a student. Never really thought of how the teachers felt."

She rolled her eyes and grinned up at him. He swallowed hard, wondering why he couldn't get his mind off her lips tonight.

"No one ever does. And, here we are. It's chillier than I thought it was."

He tugged her close as they made their way to the front of his house. "I should have given you my coat."

She shrugged as she pulled away, letting him open the front door. "I have my own on. I'm not that cold, Loch. Winter isn't over yet, but it's not that bad at the moment."

"Bite your tongue, woman. Don't encourage Mother Nature. Now, where is your laptop?"

"I've got it. Thanks for this, Loch. I need to get a few things done if I want to make my date tomorrow."

Loch froze. Surely, he'd heard her wrong.

"Date?"

Ainsley turned and gave him a look that could have peeled paint off the wall. "Yes. A date. I haven't accepted as of yet, but a friend asked me out, and I said I'd let him know tonight if I was free. Got a problem with that, Loch?"

He stuffed his hands into his pockets, wondering how he'd fucked everything up so badly again. "Didn't know you were dating."

"You never asked. I date, Loch."

"Not often." He winced as she punched his shoulder. "I didn't mean it like that."

"You're an idiot. I've already told you that tonight, but I figured I'd say it again. I don't date often because I don't have time, not because I'm not desirable."

His brows shot up. "Whoa, I didn't say that. I didn't even mention anything like that. Now, who is this guy? And why am I just now hearing about him?"

"You're fucking kidding me right now. Seriously? Does

it matter? I don't tell you everything, Loch. And don't act so surprised someone actually asked me out. Maybe if you actually *saw* me, you wouldn't be so surprised."

"I see you." He whispered the words, but he wasn't sure she'd heard him.

"Maybe if you saw me as someone other than your friend, someone who isn't just the one who's always here, you'd actually see that I'm dateable. I've seen the way you look at me when I'm near other men. Like that one night when you thought I was with Fox. And yet you do *nothing* about it. You stand there and act surprised that I'm going on a date, yet you won't even look at me. You don't *see* me."

Loch growled low before taking a step closer to her. "I see you, Ainsley. That's the fucking problem."

Then, he took her mouth with his and knew he'd made a mistake at the first touch.

But she didn't back away.

And neither did he.

Chapter 2

*L*och knew he should back away from Ainsley, but at that first, sweet taste of whiskey and woman, he knew he was addicted.

He'd never kissed Ainsley before.

Never allowed himself to get this close.

Never allowed himself to even think about it.

Now, it was all he could think about because she was in his arms, and his mouth was on hers. He knew he should back away and forget that this ever happened.

But he couldn't.

Ainsley pulled away first, but he was the one to take two steps back, his chest heaving. He could still taste her on his tongue, still craved her.

"What…what was *that?*" Her words came out with a bit of a bite, and he knew he'd deserve it if she punched him in the gut—or worse.

"You said I didn't see you," he growled out. "I *see* you, Ainsley. And like I said, that's the problem."

He'd repeated the words, yet he still didn't know what they meant. Not really. He needed to figure out what the hell was going on in his head. But it was as if something had come over him. He hadn't been able to hold back from acting on the thoughts that had been in the back of his mind for longer than he cared to admit.

Ainsley's chest rose and fell as she stared at him, and he couldn't help but notice the hard points of her nipples pressing against her shirt. He'd done his best not to look before, to never allow the parts of her that were *woman* enter his mind for fear that it would ruin it all.

Ainsley was his…everything. Damn it. His best friend. His confidante. Part of his soul.

She couldn't be more.

Not when he'd fuck it all up and ruin whatever they had on a chance that could never work out.

He wasn't the guy women loved for long. They left when they got tired. His job, his *past* was too hard for them. They weren't safe.

Ainsley, *his* Ainsley, wouldn't be safe.

She shook her head then took a step toward him.

He didn't move back.

"You can't just…you can't just change things." She was right in front of him now, so close he could feel the heat of her on his skin. There was something in her expression he couldn't make out, and it worried him because he could *always* read her face.

At least he thought he could.

Maybe he'd been wrong this entire time.

Maybe he was wrong now.

Loch didn't know what to say, but when she put her hand on his chest, he knew he'd be making one more mistake tonight.

Throwing caution to the wind, he lowered his head, took her mouth, and lost himself in her.

She didn't pull away, didn't take a step back. Instead, she put her other hand on Loch's chest, her fingernails digging into his shirt. Their kiss was rough, needy, all tongues and teeth.

Somehow, he pushed her back to the couch, needing more of her. Her hands moved to his back, sliding up under his shirt so her skin was on his.

"More," she breathed, and he growled.

"Done."

Then, he had his hands on her ass, lifting her up so she sat on the edge of the couch, her legs spread, and his body fitting firmly between her thighs. He wanted her pants off, her clothes in a heap beside them. He wanted to be inside her, wanted to touch her, wanted to *know* her.

She bit his jaw, and he moved a bit to take her mouth, his hands roaming over her body. She wrapped her legs around his waist, arching into him when he gently bit down on her neck.

"Loch."

He liked his name on her lips. Wanted more of it. When he tugged on the bottom of her shirt, she lifted her arms above her head so he could strip it off. Then, he was staring down at her bra-clad breasts, his mouth watering as he finally gazed where he'd told himself never to look.

He cupped one full breast in his hand, his thumb gently grazing her nipple through the lace, and met her gaze. He didn't say anything, wasn't sure he could. And since she didn't say anything either, Loch figured they were both thinking the same thing.

One word could shatter the moment.

One word could remind them both that this was a bad fucking idea.

So, he didn't say a damn word.

And neither did she.

He leaned down, kissed between her breasts, sucked on her nipples through her bra before reaching around to undo the clasp. Her breasts fell heavily into his hands, and he covered them with kisses, licks, and attention. She moaned, her hand running through his hair, reminding him that he needed to get a haircut.

That thought was cut short when she raked her nails down his back, reminding him where he was and exactly what he was doing. He needed more of her, needed *all* of her. He shifted their position so her feet were on the ground and he could pull down her pants. She helped him, working on his shirt and belt at the same time. Soon, they were both standing naked in front of each other, years of history and who they were to one another pulsating between them even as they ignored it.

Then, they were on the couch, his body hovering over

hers as he kissed her again, her legs spread, and his lower body pressed firmly to hers. He didn't move, didn't thrust, not when he wanted to savor.

But Ainsley apparently wasn't about to let him go slow.

She trailed her foot down the back of his calf, pressing him closer to her. He pulled away slightly, knowing they needed a condom before they did anything. Instead, he slid down her body, leaving kisses and long licks along the way.

When he settled himself between her legs, he groaned then spread her with his fingers so he could study her down below. He looked up into her face, and she stared back at him with hooded eyes, licking her lips.

"I have a condom in my purse."

He wasn't going to think about the whys of that, so he gave her a tight nod then lowered his head, taking her into his mouth. She bucked as he sucked on her clit, licking along her slit and using his fingers to tease her. She shook under him, under his care, and when she came on his face, he didn't stop licking at her cunt, wanting her to go over the edge one more time before he took her.

Hard.

When she came down for the second time, her sweetness was branded on his tongue. He stood up, his cock bouncing against his stomach. He made his way to her purse, rummaging around until he found the single condom tucked into a pocket. He turned back to her, opening the package and sliding the condom over his length as he met her gaze.

She swallowed hard, her chest rising as she sucked in a

breath. Loch couldn't help but watch the way her pink-tipped breasts rose and fell as she did so. It made his mouth water. All he wanted to do was fill her, be with her, have her as his.

And because Loch knew he'd look into her eyes as he filled her and, if he weren't careful, fuck everything up more than he already had, he prowled toward her, took her hips in his hands, and flipped her over onto her stomach. She let out a gasp then gripped the edge of the couch, looking over her shoulder at him.

He'd known she was beautiful, had done his best to ignore that fact the entire time he'd known her. But right then, with her eyes dark with pleasure, her lips swollen from his kisses, and her body arched, ready for him, he knew he'd never forget this moment for as long as he lived.

Then, he was on her, his hands digging into her hips as he slid inside.

Bliss.

Pure fucking bliss.

She was his drug, his agony, his everything.

He pushed even deeper, their breaths coming in pants as he tried not to think about the meaning of the thoughts that had just rushed through his mind.

Ainsley's head fell back, and he slid in and out of her, slowly at first since she was so damn tight and hot that he didn't want to hurt her. Then, faster. Soon, he was pounding in and out of her, her lush ass pushing back at him, meeting him thrust for thrust. He slid one hand around in front of her, sliding a finger over her swollen clit peeking out from below its hood.

Then, she came again, squeezing his cock, and he couldn't hold back anymore. He slammed into her without abandon, sweat sliding down the middle of his back as he took her, branded her, marked her. And when he came, he shouted her name, one hand on her breast, the other probably leaving bruises on her hip.

As Loch fought to catch his breath, he lay next to Ainsley and wondered what the fuck they were going to do next. The fact that he'd slept with Ainsley without thinking of the consequences of his actions, of *their* actions, told him that he was the asshole she'd called him earlier in the evening.

"I need to go." Ainsley suddenly shot up, pulling on her clothes as she practically scurried away from him.

"Ainsley." He hated talking, hated sharing his feelings and what he was thinking, but he couldn't let the best thing in his life—other than his daughter—walk out of the house as if she'd done something wrong.

Because if anyone had done anything wrong, it was him.

It was always him.

"Don't. I need to get home and work and…and…fuck it, Loch. I need to think." She turned then, wearing only her pants and a bra as she stared at him. "Let me think, because I have no idea what just happened."

He stood up then, taking care of the condom in a tissue before pulling up his jeans. "I don't know either."

"And words like that aren't helping, so I'm going to go, get some sleep, and maybe, in the morning, we'll figure out what the hell just happened. Because we've never done that before, and from the way you're looking at me, I don't know if you regret it already or not."

He didn't say anything. He didn't have the words. Ainsley's expression fell.

"I see."

"Ainsley." She didn't see. *He* didn't, so how could she?

"Don't. Don't say anything. I can't deal with this right now and, frankly, I don't think either of us should." She looked up again when she was fully dressed. He could see the pain in her eyes, and he had no idea how to fix it.

He always fixed things.

But he didn't know if he could fix *them*.

Ainsley didn't say another word and, because he was just as lost as she apparently was, he let her walk out the door without stopping her. He hadn't meant to kiss her, hadn't meant to touch her, hadn't meant to learn what she felt like beneath him.

And yet, he had. And now they both had to deal with what happened next.

He could still taste her on his tongue, and he didn't want to wash it down with whiskey or beer. Instead, he pulled on the rest of his clothes, grabbed his gear, and headed to his gym. He'd work off the feelings racing inside him at what felt like a thousand miles per hour.

He'd never let himself think of Ainsley as anything more than his best friend before, and that had been for a

22

reason. He didn't do relationships. He fucked them up and pushed people away. He'd had to do it in his old job—to keep them safe, and to keep himself safe, as well.

Loch needed Ainsley in his life, he had for years. Because she was his rock, his anchor. He knew it wasn't fair to either of them for him to only think of her that way. Besides, what could he give her?

Nothing.

Not to mention, he could ruin Ainsley's relationship with his daughter if he pursued anything with Ainsley. So, he'd ignore what happened. Act as if everything were fine, and the two of them could just move on.

It had been a mistake.

It couldn't happen again.

He'd bury what he was feeling about their night deep down and hope to hell and back Ainsley didn't hate him come morning.

He already hated himself enough.

Loch stuffed his hands into his pockets as the temperature dropped with the setting of the sun and walked the few blocks to his gym. He could have driven, but he needed the walk and the cool air to clear his head. He couldn't get Ainsley from his mind. She'd always been there, but never like this.

Damn it.

As soon as he turned the corner, he immediately knew something was wrong. Lights from two police cars blinked at him, and he could see where they were parked.

Right in front of his gym.

His pulse raced as he jogged forward. There was a barricade up, and he couldn't get through, but he could hear well enough to know that something was wrong.

Deadly wrong.

"We found the body in the back," one of the officers whispered to another. "We better call in homicide. I don't know if we can handle this ourselves. There's never been a murder in Whiskey before."

Body.

Murder.

And all near Loch's damn gym.

He knew all about dead bodies, had seen more than he could count in his life. But he had a feeling this one would hit too close to home. It had already. Literally. Chills broke out over his skin, and he prayed to God that it wasn't someone he knew.

He quickly messaged his family in a group text to see if they were okay, grateful they each responded saying "goodnight." He didn't mention why he'd texted, nor did he text Ainsley as he'd just seen her, but he swallowed hard, knowing that this was only the beginning.

There had been a murder in Whiskey.

And from the look on the officer's face, Loch had a feeling he was going to be in the middle of it all.

Again.

Chapter 3

*A*insley Harris really wanted a stiff drink and a nap, but even after a long day at school, she knew she wasn't about to get that anytime soon. The whole campus had been abuzz about the dead body and the potential murder in Whiskey the night before, and keeping her students' attention on chemical bonds and not on their phones had taken all of her energy and patience.

It had been worse with the teachers during their breaks, with so many wondering who had been killed, and trying to do the math as to whom was missing. The authorities and news cycles were keeping a tight lid on things, but Ainsley knew that could change any minute. Murder in small, tourist towns tended to wreak havoc.

Ainsley's heart hurt for whoever it was and whatever had happened, but a small part of her was relieved that it wasn't any of her friends. She only knew that because she'd texted or spoken to each of them the night before after she heard, or this morning before work, and all of them had checked back in.

Even Loch.

She pressed her lips together, pushing thoughts of him from her mind.

The students were home or on their way home, and the doors of the building would be locked in five minutes, so she only had half that to pack up the rest of her things and head to her car before starting the next phase of her day: working outside of her classroom on grading and lesson plans. Her school didn't actually like it when teachers did that on campus, so they kicked them out. Ainsley had always found that odd since the work that piled up was because of the administration and so on. But, apparently, paying for electricity after so-called *work hours* wasn't on their agenda.

Ainsley didn't mind working at home, though. Or at Loch's house, since she did a lot of her grading there, as well.

She paused in her packing, her throat going dry and her thighs clamping together at the thought of Loch.

Nope, not going to think about that.

Him.

Not going to think about him.

Or that.

Where was she?

Oh, right, she'd been thinking about grading. That was nice and safe and took most of her energy, but as her mother had always said, she was Ainsley Harris and had a lot of energy to burn. She worked her ass off, and sometimes even got weekends off to spend time with her friends. She took cooking classes because her skills were abysmal—at least, before—was taking a dance class with her new friend Melody at the new dance studio in town, and sometimes she even went out on dates with nice guys with bright smiles—who did absolutely nothing for her.

And they really did nothing for her, to her, or even *with* her in most cases because she was in love with her best friend.

She was the cliché of clichés, and she was pretty sure every single person in her life except for the man himself knew.

But because she was a big girl with big-girl panties, she did her best to never let it be an issue. It *couldn't* be. She focused on work, her friends that were her only family left —at least that's what it felt like most days even though she still had her mom in her life, albeit somewhat removed because of her own issues and grief. She missed her sister so much some days it hurt to breathe, yet she kept going. But she wasn't going off on *that* tangent at the moment. And, sometimes, she even focused on her sad little dating life.

Like her night out with the sweet man she'd skipped out on. She had called the night before after the *incident* and had backed out of their date this evening as politely as she could. It wasn't as if she could sit in front of him at Marsha Brown's over delicious gumbo and act as if she hadn't had her hand down her best friend's pants, or her mouth on his, or his dick inside her as he made her come not once but many times the night before.

Yeah, that wasn't going to happen. And since she was currently *still* frozen at her desk thinking about said dick and all its magical dick powers, she shut down those thoughts as quickly as she'd shut Loch down the night before when he wanted to freaking *talk* after whatever the hell had happened. Instead, she packed the last of her things.

She ran down the empty hall, thankful that none of her students were there to witness that fact since she'd given a few of them a stern warning just that day about running in the halls like a lunatic. Thanks to the myriad thoughts she shouldn't be having, she was running late, and there was someone far more important than her or Loch waiting on her.

The person who meant the world to both of them and who, therefore, guaranteed the incident of the night before should never be repeated or talked about.

Because if Ainsley had to talk about the fact that she'd made a horrible mistake and given in to the one need she'd hidden for so long, she'd break. And she'd broken enough in her life, thank you very much.

She didn't want to break down over Loch Collins.

She'd just bury that need and memory down deep and ignore it until it festered. And then she'd stuff it down again. That was the right thing to do when it came to a four-year-old girl who meant the world to Ainsley—if not the most healthy and mature course of action.

Ainsley got into her car and shivered a bit from the wind that seemed to come out of nowhere, but since it was Whiskey, Pennsylvania, it had probably been there all day. Then she started her way to Loch's to relieve his mom of Misty duty.

Ainsley turned the corner as a smile played on her lips, thinking of the little girl who lit up her life. When Loch and Marnie dated, Ainsley hadn't thought much of it since Loch was pretty secretive about his personal life—she never called it a *love life* because Ainsley had boundaries and her mental health to care for—and the man hadn't truly seemed serious about the other woman. He'd gone on trips often for his job with the old firm she didn't know much about, but when he *was* in town, it was always for short periods where he seemed to spend as much time with Ainsley as he did with Marnie.

It hadn't mattered that Ainsley had feelings for him. It truly didn't. Because those feelings were never allowed to interfere with the fact that Loch was her best friend. She trusted him with everything.

Almost everything, she corrected herself.

She didn't trust him with her heart, but that wasn't something that would ever change, so she did her best to not think about it at all.

She reminded herself once again that she wasn't going to think about him. Remember?

"Easier said than done," she muttered under her breath as she turned down Main Street.

The town was in full winter bloom with tourists, and because a few streets were cordoned off thanks to an upcoming festival and parade, she'd had to take Main Street through town. Not that full bloom in winter was huge, it was still technically their downtime and had less tourists and cars than any other time of the year. She drove past Dare's bar and inn, then past the street that held Fox's paper. Then past Loch's gym and Melody's studio. There was the ice cream place she loved that even had booming business in February. And the other restaurants and art galleries, the tattoo shops and trinket shops.

Ainsley drove past the old church, the bridge that covered the waterfall, and the huge red barn that housed the small theatre company.

People were bustling, going from place to place, though not as many as there could be since most were still working and it was cold. But, honestly, Ainsley was glad to see the crowds.

News that someone had died in Whiskey had broken, and she had been afraid that people would be too scared to come to town.

She didn't know what would happen in the coming days or weeks if the person wasn't caught—if it *was* a murder—or if and when the news came out that it was only an accident. Whiskey relied on tourism, and she knew the town's residents were thinking about that while, at the same time, they were worried about the poor soul who had lost their life—as well as the fact that a killer could still be out there.

Ainsley shook her head and turned once more on the way to Loch's home, wondering how her brain could be going so many different directions.

Whiskey was family, and yet the town was growing.

Perhaps she needed to worry about what could be coming next and if she might be left behind.

Ainsley turned off her car and sighed after she'd parked beside Loch's mother's car. She knew there were dangers in the world, horrible things that happened to good people. She'd witnessed it with Kenzie and Melody recently, and she knew that Loch had done things in his past that he was still closed-off about. Yet the idea that someone could be killed in her town felt like something that should never happen.

Apparently, she was naive, but she liked that naivety.

Loch's mom opened the door as soon as Ainsley got to the porch and she sank into the woman's arms. Barbara Collins gave amazing hugs—something the woman had apparently gifted to her sons and daughter.

Ainsley had been on the receiving end of the hugs from the Collins siblings enough times in her life to know that she was wanted, needed, and thought of as part of their family.

Not that she necessarily felt that way about Loch at that moment, but thinking about that while in his mother's arms probably wasn't the best.

"You look good, hon," Mrs. Collins said as she let go of

Ainsley and took a step back. "Come on in. Misty is washing her hands after her snack. I need to head home now, but now that you're on shift, she should be set until Loch comes home for dinner. It took four years, but we have our system down."

Ainsley just smiled, shaking her head as she stepped into Loch's home, taking off her shoes and jacket after setting her things down on the table nearest the door. Mrs. Collins closed the front door behind them, keeping the warm air in the house and the chill from the outside far enough away that it was almost a memory.

"You say that, but full-day classes are coming with the next school year. Plus dance lessons with Melody and the new assistant she hired to help when she has the baby. Then there's bound to be teams and other lessons and numerous after-school activities because Misty loves to do everything and anything she can so she can learn it all."

Mrs. Collins just smiled. "Sounds like someone else I know."

Ainsley tilted her head to the side, confused. "Loch? I don't remember if he did all of that as a kid. I was way younger than him and didn't really start becoming friends with all of you until after high school."

She was a full eight years younger than Loch, meaning she'd had a crush on him as young girls do with the older guys with the dark looks and wicked smiles. Then she'd found other boys her age and had forgotten Loch for a time.

Perhaps not quite forgotten, he'd always been there.

But it wasn't until she graduated high school and was in college, still living in Whiskey since she hadn't been able to afford dorms or other apartment pricing away from her town, that she'd really gotten to know Loch and the rest of the family.

She'd been friends with Tabby throughout high school and had even been in the same grade as Loch's sister, but once the other woman left Whiskey for college out in Denver, eventually staying and meeting the love of her life, Ainsley had gravitated toward Loch. Not just because of a crush she'd had as a little girl with a dream, but because they'd gelled. In jest, the family always said that she and Loch had been best friends since forever, but they really hadn't been. It had only been about ten years or so. But that seemed like a lifetime to Ainsley.

Mrs. Collins shook her head as the two of them made their way into the living room. "I was actually talking about you."

Ainsley frowned. "Me? Misty doesn't take after me." After all, she wasn't the little girl's mother, something she reminded herself often when it came to certain things like bedtime, watching Misty grow up, or even when thinking about Loch.

There was a fine line between helpful and delusional when it came to how she interacted with Loch's family and, sometimes, she wasn't sure which side she stood on.

"I think she does. You're the one taking dance and cooking classes. In high school, you did track, swimming, cheerleading, math team, and a few other academic things

I can't name off the top of my head. You've always done so much. You want to learn all the things, just like Misty." The other woman reached out and squeezed Ainsley's hand. "It's not genetics that makes a child become who they are, not really. You're here with us day in and day out with that little girl, Misty's bound to pick up a few of your traits."

Ainsley swallowed hard, trying not to think about the fact that if she and Loch ever actually talked about what had happened the night before, he might push her out of Misty's life altogether. She might be forced out of Loch's life altogether. Ainsley's palms went damp, her mind going a little fuzzy as the ramifications hit her full-on. She was grateful that Mrs. Collins had let go of her hand or Ainsley would be in trouble. The older woman saw everything. And from the way she was looking at Ainsley, she was afraid she saw too much now, too.

"You should get going, or you're going to be late," Ainsley said quickly, ignoring the conversation they were in the middle of. She wasn't doing a good job of tracking her thoughts, and if she weren't careful, she'd spill it all to Mrs. Collins—and then her life might as well be over.

"I'm on my way out the door as we speak, but Ainsley, dear, are you okay?"

Ainsley smiled widely, hoping it reached her eyes and not in the manic way she felt at the moment. "I'm fine. Really. Long day at school and I'm ready for the weekend."

"Aren't we all. But if you need to talk, honey, I'm here."

"Ainsley!"

She turned at the best sound in the world and crouched down. Misty ran into her arms, and she hugged the little girl tight, her eyes closing as she remembered how truly thankful she was that she had this family and this child in particular in her life.

Misty smelled of soap and chocolate, meaning Grandma must have snuck in a few cookies right after school. Loch wasn't a fan of that since they all tried to watch their sugar intake and the man *did* own a gym, after all, but Ainsley knew Mrs. Collins only did it on the occasional Friday.

"You're here," Misty whispered. "I'm so glad you're here."

Tears stung Ainsley's eyes, and she did her best to blink them away before they dared to fall down her cheeks. Mrs. Collins didn't need to see them, nor did the little girl in Ainsley's arms.

"I'm glad I am, too." She kissed Misty's cheek before standing up, keeping her hand in Misty's. "Want to say goodbye to your grandma before she goes home?"

Misty grinned widely and then scampered over to hug her grandma goodbye. Ainsley knew Mrs. Collins was probably the world's proudest grandmother—a title Ainsley's mother would never want nor care to use. Not that Ainsley was a mother yet, but for some reason, her mind was going to strange places tonight even *thinking* about her mom and everything they likely wouldn't share. But Mrs. Collins had Loch's daughter, Dare's son, Tabby's upcoming birth, as well as Fox's newly announced pregnancy with Melody. Ainsley had a feeling Kenzie would be joining the ranks soon, making Dare a dad two times over. Soon, there would be twice as many Collinses in Whiskey as there had been before.

And Ainsley would forever be the best friend.

The place she needed to stay because *this* was her family, the people she loved and clung to. Because they were who she needed, and she did her best to do right by them. Doing whatever she'd done with Loch in their moment of weakness and passion wasn't something to be repeated.

Not if she wanted to keep living the life she'd built for herself.

Not if she wanted to keep her best friend in her life.

"Oh, Misty, why don't you get your art project out to show Ainsley and then your dad when he gets home? I'll just say goodbye to Ainsley now, okay?"

"Okay, Grandma. Love you!" Misty ran off, and Ainsley just smiled. Misty was in a good mood today, and that meant loads of energy for both of them.

"I just wanted her away so I could tell you to be careful when you leave tonight after Loch gets home," Mrs. Collins whispered. "I haven't heard much about what happened last night, but *because* there isn't much news, and not even Fox has let anything slip, it has to be serious."

Ainsley nodded. "I know. Do you think they'll release the deceased's name today?"

"I think they'll have to. But, Ainsley? I do know that they found the body in back of Loch's gym."

Ainsley froze, tongue going dry. "Loch..."

"I don't know anything more. Honestly. Ask him for any information if you can. You know him. If it was near his place, he's going to take it personally and bottle it all up and try to take care of everything all on his own. He's not a cop, and neither is Dare anymore, but all my boys like to fix things."

Ainsley gave the woman a tight hug. "I'll be careful, but you, as well. I know it sounds horrible, but I hope it's a one-off thing and they figure it out soon. I don't like the idea that there's danger in Whiskey."

"I know, dear. I know. Tell Loch I love him, as I love you. And tell him to call his mother." And with that, the other woman left the house and headed to her car. Though it was still daylight, Ainsley locked the door behind her and kept her eyes on the street through the window as Mrs. Collins drove away.

As soon as the car was out of sight, Ainsley let out a breath and rubbed the goosebumps on her arms. Talking about murder wasn't something she was a fan of, not when it was truly real. She loved to watch true crime shows and listened to podcasts about real-life events, but she particularly liked the solved cases where the bad guy had been caught and was put away for a very long time. She didn't like that something had happened in her town. It might make her hypocritical, but she was always aware when she watched those shows and listened to the stories. She cared for the victim, not whoever had committed the crime. The victims and their families were the ones that mattered in the end, though not everyone felt that way.

As the sound of Misty coming back into the living room reached her ears, she pasted another smile on her face and went to hang out with the little girl who would be her focus for the next hour or so. It wasn't her night to cook—she and Loch had decided they'd take turns on the nights she was with Misty and he worked late but got off in time for dinner. So, that meant she didn't have to leave from her spot on Loch's very comfy couch unless she wanted.

And she wasn't going to think about the last time she'd been on the couch with him.

At all.

"Are you okay? You're all red."

Ainsley blinked and patted her cheek. "I'm fine. Just...uh, hot."

"It's cold outside, but we can go out there if you want," Misty said, wiggling off the couch. Ainsley leaned forward and tapped Misty's ankle.

"I'm fine. Just a hot flash. Women get those, you know."

Misty's eyes widened. "Grandma has them. So does other grandma, but I don't think she likes them as much because she always mutters about them under her breath." *Other grandma* being Marnie's mother. That set of grandparents saw Misty at least once a month, and though the interactions were always awkward for Loch and made him grumpy as hell, the couple was good to Misty. It was horrible that Loch's ex had walked out on not only Misty's life but also Loch's and Marnie's parents, but somehow, everyone was making it work. Even if it wasn't always easy.

"Will I get hot flashes?" Misty asked, then turned back to the television.

Ainsley really didn't want to get into the whole menopause talk but, thankfully, Misty moved the conversation over to a new cartoon about a robot and his friends that was based off a movie. One that had made Ainsley cry all over Loch's shoulder when they'd seen it in the theatre. Children's movies were not supposed to make you sob but, apparently, that's all they seemed to do for Ainsley these days.

She and Misty were just finishing up one episode when the sound of the front door opening pulled both of their attention from the TV. Ainsley turned it off quickly as Misty ran to her father with as much, if not more, enthusiasm than she had when she'd first seen Ainsley earlier.

"I take it you had a good day?" Loch asked, his voice low but his smile wide and reaching his eyes. It was only when he looked up at Ainsley that the smile faltered, and his eyes went a little duller than they had been before.

This wasn't a conversation she and Loch were going to have with his daughter around, and from the look on his face, it wasn't a conversation he wanted to have anytime soon. So, instead of acting like an adult and finding a way to talk to him civilly and privately, she packed up her things and kissed the top of Misty's head in goodbye.

"I need to head out. Lots of work to do this weekend." She pointedly looked at Misty rather than Loch, afraid of what she'd see on his face.

"No dinner?" Misty asked, her lower lip in a bit of a pout before she sucked it back in. Loch hated when Misty tried that act, and Ainsley agreed. Apparently, Marnie had used it often, and that was a whole other level of things Ainsley didn't want to think about just then.

"Next time. Promise." Ainsley held back the wince at the promise. If Loch pushed her out of his life, if they didn't find a way to make their friendship continue working after what had happened, that might not be a promise she could keep.

Ainsley finally met Loch's gaze and lifted her chin. "Have a good night, Loch."

"Need me to drive you home? It's getting dark now."

She ignored the way the deep growl of his voice simultaneously sent shivers down her spine and brought tears to her eyes.

"I'm okay. I'm just going from your driveway to my garage."

"Text when you get home."

"Always do."

Because he worried. That was Loch. A worrier. And never one for doing things out of the blue without a plan. That was just one reason she knew that what had happened between them could never happen again.

Just one of many reasons.

When she got into her car, she knew Loch watched her

from his window. Only she didn't think it was because he couldn't look away. No, it was because he took care of those in his circle. He always had, and he always would.

She was just one of his.

One of many.

Never…never the only one.

And she'd get used to that. After all, she had been fine with it for over a decade. Or she pretended to be. What was one more lifetime in her purgatory?

Chapter 4

*D*ennis Chamberlin.

Loch knew the name before he'd been questioned, but he hadn't known until just then what he would do if he heard it spoken aloud in this context. He knew Dennis. Had trained the other man himself. Had set his work hours, had talked to him the day Dennis died. And yet Loch hadn't been there when the man had spoken his last word, had taken his last breath.

Loch hadn't been there.

He'd been too late.

Again. And now it looked as if the man might have been killed, and everything pointed to Loch as being the guilty party.

He bit the inside of his cheek so he wouldn't cry out, wouldn't scream at the injustice of it all. Instead, he stood in his windowless office at the gym and wondered what the hell would happen next.

Dennis had been one of Loch's best trainers at the gym. He'd come to work on time, he'd stayed late if needed. He'd never hit on any of the guests or made them feel uncomfortable. He'd always worked with both men and women, not scoping out the younger, hotter versions of either sex like some of his trainers had tried to do in the past. He'd cared about those he worked with, and Loch had liked him.

And now, the other man was dead, and there was nothing Loch could do about it.

"Knock knock," Dare said as he stuck his head into Loch's office. "Thought I'd catch you here."

Loch narrowed his eyes at his brother. "I thought the door was locked."

"I'd make a joke about Loch and locking, but this isn't the time for that. And, yeah, you locked the front door to the gym, but I have a key, remember? We all have keys to our places in case of emergency." Dare moved fully into the office, closing the door behind him. Though the two of them were the only people in the building, Loch appreciated the privacy.

"And what constitutes an emergency today?" Loch asked, folding his arms over his chest.

Dare leaned against the door, mirroring Loch's movement with his arms. "Oh, I don't know, the fact that Dennis is dead and, apparently, he either died on your property in the back or was moved there. I know the police asked you a few questions last night when you stopped by since you told me, but I can bet you they'll ask a few more."

Loch knew as much. "I figured. Even if I'm not a suspect—which, who knows what the hell the local detectives will be thinking on that point, especially given the pointed questions they asked me last night—they're going to want to talk to me some more. Hell, I want to talk to them. Dennis had no family. He came to Whiskey with a group of friends about three years ago and stayed when he fell in love with the town. I hired him soon after, and he's been my best trainer since."

"That's a long time, Loch. I'm sorry he's gone."

"I'm sorry, too. And pissed the fuck off that someone would dare end his life. If it really was a murder. He's younger than us." Loch paused. "*Was* younger than us. Jesus Christ. I've seen people die, Dare. Same as you. Our old lives didn't allow us to think the best of the world. Hell, same with Fox and his work, even if he tries to find the best in his writing. But this? On our doorstep? I felt like we left our old lives because we thought Whiskey was safe. It was a fucking delusion."

Dare shook his head. "Not a delusion. We might have thought it was *safer* but never safe. I almost lost Kenzie because it wasn't safe. Fuck, Fox almost lost Melody because of the same thing. People make a place dangerous. And no matter how much you try to wall yourself off from them, they're still around you. You work in security, Loch. You might have this gym, but your manager runs it most of the time. Your other job adding and providing security systems for those in town is what makes you the money. And that tells us both you've never really thought Whiskey was that safe. Nowhere is."

Dare was right, but Loch wasn't a fan of being reminded that his brother was sometimes smarter than he was. He couldn't help it, they were all competitive.

"Just because I want to keep my family and friends safe doesn't mean I'm prepared for shit like this."

Dare nodded. "I get it. I was a cop, remember? You're the one who added all the security for my house and at the inn. Shit, I don't know if I'd be as comfortable having Kenzie alone at the house or the inn as much as she is without your security system. And, yeah, that makes me an alpha male with too much testosterone, but whatever. After everything that happened to her before we got together and right when we started seeing each other, I get overprotective."

"I'm just surprised she's not wrapped in bubble wrap and attached to your hip."

"Don't think I didn't ask."

"At least you asked. That's a step up from demanding."

Dare's eyes went dark, and Loch knew it wasn't about him but Kenzie's ex. "I'll never demand. Not from Kenzie. Not after the shit her ex pulled. But it's all connected, Loch. We're keeping those we love safe, and the fact that someone came in and hurt a friend, fucking *killed* a friend, pisses me the fuck off. Add to that the fact that you're actually connected to him and it seems very suspicious that things seem to be pointing to you, and I just have a feeling we haven't seen the end of this. You know?"

Loch nodded, his gut rolling. "I know." He'd been feeling the same. Something was off about the whole situation, and not just that Dennis was dead. Loch had seen too much in his life, had been part of too much not to have a hinky feeling about the whole thing. He just wasn't sure what he could do about it. Wasn't sure what there *was* to do about it. Dare wasn't a cop anymore. Loch didn't work for his old company anymore. They had no jurisdiction, no power to do anything except wait and see.

He just hated not having the option to do anything about it.

"You have an alibi, though." It wasn't a question, but Loch had a feeling Dare was still asking. And, yeah, Loch had an alibi if the time of death were near when they found the body. They didn't know yet, those details hadn't been released.

He'd been with his family.

And after that…he'd been with Ainsley.

But Loch wasn't sure what the hell he was going to do if someone asked.

"I do." He didn't elaborate. Didn't need to. Dare just nodded, a question in his gaze, but he didn't say more. They were brothers, they knew when they needed to share. But for now, they were allowed to keep their secrets. It would likely be different with Fox, but Loch understood that Fox liked to know everything so he could try and fix it.

"Then you're good." Dare cursed, and Loch just stared

at him. "No, you're not good. Sorry. I can't believe Dennis is dead. And I seriously can't believe his name was *just* released to Fox."

Loch nodded. "I know. Word's out, and soon it's going to be even more of a mess as they try to figure out who's responsible."

"They don't think it was an accident? They're sure it's murder?"

Loch shrugged. "They didn't tell me much, but from what I could gather, his neck was broken, and his body was found at the bottom of the stairs behind the building."

Dare's eyebrows shot up. "You heard all that? Sounds like those details should have been kept quiet."

"Two of the newer deputies were talking within earshot. I heard they got reprimanded by their boss once everyone realized I was near. Those details will probably be let out today anyway. Fox has a story on his hands."

The brothers met gazes, both frowning. "Fox hates writing the horrors without the light," Dare said softly. "You know that." Dare looked down again, putting his hands on his hips as he seemingly ordered his thoughts. Loch just stared at him, his mind going down its own path.

Loch nodded. "That's why he stayed in Whiskey instead of going somewhere else with more breaking news." Fox had stayed in Whiskey to write what mattered to the town as well as to keep their people informed of what was going on in the world. Their younger brother had always been good at keeping the balance, but death and murder was a whole other thing. Fox could handle it, though, of that Loch was sure. His brother could deal with anything.

"Well, he's going to be full of news soon I think."

"Hopefully, they'll catch the bastard," Loch growled out.

"I don't have that many connections to the department here, but I'll do my best to find out more. Especially if they really think you have anything to do with this."

"Just don't put a target on your back because you're poking your head where you're not wanted," Loch warned.

"I could say the same," Dare drawled. "Now, come on over to the bar. We'll go have lunch and get out of this place since it's closed. You going to open tomorrow?"

"Unless there's an issue, yeah. I could have opened today according to the department, but it didn't feel right. You know?"

Dare met his gaze. "I do. Let's get some food and figure out what the hell we're going to do next." His brother moved from the door and went to open it. "I know I didn't ask, and I'm not really asking at all. Come to lunch, Loch. You lost your friend. Even if he wasn't really a friend and just someone you knew and hired. You still lost him. And we both know this isn't the end of the story."

Loch sighed but moved toward the door as Dare opened it. "You've sure gotten deep since you got with Kenzie."

"True. But she lets me scratch and burp when I feel like I'm getting in touch with my emotions too much."

"Classy," Loch said with a snort as they made their way outside.

Loch's snort was probably the first thing the detective saw as he stepped out of his car, and Loch stiffened ever so slightly when he saw the other man.

"Well, here we go."

"Loch Collins?"

Loch stopped in front of his gym, Dare by his side. His brother had his phone out and was either calling a family member, their lawyer, or getting ready to record the interaction. Knowing Dare, he'd find a way to make all of it happen.

Plus, none of them liked Detective Renkle. He'd been an asshole to Dare and Kenzie and hadn't been the nicest to Melody either. His partner, Detective Shannon had been the nice one. Thankfully, the other detective was also getting out of the car.

"Yes, Detective Renkle. I'm Loch. We met two nights ago."

"And a few times before that," Dare added before turning slightly to speak into the phone.

Ah, the lawyer it seemed.

"We have a few questions for you," Renkle continued. "How about you come down to the station so we can talk." Again, not a question.

"Am I under arrest?" Loch asked.

Shannon shook his head. "No."

"Not at this time," Renkle added, and Loch did his best not to glare. He was a big man and looked intimidating even when he was smiling. It never helped when dealing with authorities to look like he could kick their asses. Well, it had helped when he was at his other job, but he'd usually been on the authorities' side.

Shannon glanced over at his partner before looking at Loch again. "But we have a few questions, and it would be easier if you were at the station."

Easier for whom? But Loch didn't ask that.

"Fine. We can do that. We were headed out to lunch. Is this going to take long?"

"Just cooperate, and you'll be fine," Shannon added, but Loch wasn't sure.

"We'll be there," Dare put in. "With our lawyer."

"Need a lawyer?" Renkle asked. "Something you need to tell us?"

Loch didn't say anything, but Dare answered for him.

"I was a cop, Renkle. I know our rights." Dare sounded almost bored, but Loch knew it was just a façade.

"For a cop, you sure are friendly with lawyers." Renkle's voice almost sent Loch over the edge, but he held himself back. Thankfully, so did Dare.

"Any good cop is," Dare said with a flash of a grin before he glared again. "Meet you at the station."

"You can always ride with us," Renkle sneered.

Jesus Christ, they were stuck in a bad detective movie. "Let's just get this over with. You need to figure out what happened to Dennis, and standing here like this isn't helping." He'd almost said "whipping out your dicks," but he'd refrained. Knowing Renkle, he'd find a way to put Loch behind bars for the offhand comment.

Shannon nudged Renkle back to the car, and Dare sighed beside Loch. "Knew it wasn't over."

"Nope. Not even close."

BY THE TIME Loch got home from the station, he was exhausted and hungry since he hadn't been able to get food like he'd planned. The questioning had actually gone super easily and, honestly, probably could have happened right there on the street in front of the gym since they'd only asked about Dennis's work schedule. The detectives had questioned Loch about where he was the night of the murder, and while Loch had said that he was at the bar with witnesses, he hadn't mentioned Ainsley and their time together after. If they asked his whereabouts for a specific time, then he'd tell them. But, as of now, he didn't know *when* Dennis had been killed, and he hadn't wanted to air any dirty laundry he didn't need to. Not telling the cops his entire life story might not be the best decision, but hell, he'd known too many people in his line of work who had said too much and had to deal with more issues because of it, even though they were innocent. He had a feeling the cops had no idea who killed Dennis and were only just starting their investigation. They needed to figure out Dennis first before they could figure out who killed him.

Either way, it gave Loch a headache, and he had a feeling the harder questions were coming.

Or maybe he was just overthinking because he tended to see the worst in people. Renkle notwithstanding, Loch didn't think anyone actually believed Loch was guilty.

Misty was at his parents' for the day since his mother had wanted a princess afternoon or something like that, so he had a few more hours to himself where he could get something to eat and maybe take a nap.

His phone buzzed, and he frowned at the readout. He hadn't heard from Ainsley all day, and the silence between them was only getting more awkward with each passing minute.

Ainsley: *I heard you were taken into the station! Are you okay?*

Jesus. Word traveled fast in Whiskey. Or rather, word traveled fast when it came to his family. Then again, he'd have talked to her himself if they weren't avoiding each other because of what happened the other night.

Loch: *They had a few questions about Dennis. I'm fine. You don't need to be worried.*

Ainsley: *Of course I'm worried, Loch.*

Ainsley: *I'm so sorry about Dennis.*

Loch sighed and pinched the bridge of his nose. He didn't know what to feel when it came to Ainsley. Things were so messed up, and Loch hated that he couldn't rely on the one person he'd always been able to lean on because he'd fucked up like he did. This was his fault, and he had no idea how to fix it.

Loch: *Me too.*

Ainsley: *Let me know if you need anything.*

He was about to answer that he was fine when she messaged again.

Ainsley: *And we need to talk. You know we do.*

He didn't answer that, just put his phone back into his pocket, his head aching. Yeah, they needed to talk, but he wasn't sure what they could say to each other to fix what had happened. If he were honest with himself, this had been a long time coming, and yet it still surprised the hell out of him. He had no idea what to say to her, what would help things, or what would make everything better.

He'd ruined what they had, and he was afraid there was no coming back from that.

And since he'd already made himself sick over that and the situation with Dennis that day, he knew he just needed some time to think and get his thoughts in order because if he spoke to Ainsley right then, he'd fuck it all up even more.

Loch sighed and went to check the mail he'd put on the kitchen island when he walked in. In the middle was a large manila envelope that looked out of place. He set it aside for the moment but frowned when he noticed an estate lawyer's name on the return address.

"Huh." He set it down on the counter again, got himself a beer, and took a sip as he tried to think of what an estate lawyer would be sending him. Loch's first thought was something about Dennis, but that was insane, so it had to be about something else.

He just had no idea what it could be.

He opened another letter addressed to him first, one

without a return address and figured it was junk mail, but he still needed to open it before he shredded it.

Instead, there was a single typed note in it. His hands fisted near his sides as he tried to figure out what the hell it could mean.

"It will be mine. Watch your back. Your friend already lost his life by being where he shouldn't have been. I want those papers. Too bad he was in the wrong place at the wrong time. You know who I am. You know me. You know what I want. What I need. Don't waste too much time, or your little friend might not be the only person who loses what's important."

"What the fuck?"

He looked down at the letter, unease spreading through him. He sighed, set down his beer, and opened the other large envelope. When he scanned the cover letter, he stiffened, ice sliding through his veins, and his gut churning once more.

He looked at the name listed, then read through the file, wondering how the hell he'd ended up in this other dimension. Because there was no way this was happening, not when he was dealing with Dennis, Ainsley, Misty, and so many other things in his life.

No fucking way.

Jason Kincaid was dead.

Jason fucking Kincaid.

His mentor, friend, and the one who'd helped him get his head on straight when he hadn't known what to do with his life. He'd been the company's owner, the one who'd trained them all and kept everyone safe. He'd been the one to help Loch figure out what the hell to do once he decided not to work with the company anymore and needed to stay home to be a dad.

Jason had helped him with so fucking much.

And now, the man was dead.

But, apparently, Loch hadn't known him as well as he thought because Jason had left the company to Loch. *To do with as you please.*

In other words, to dismantle it because there was no way Loch was going to be the boss. Not with that group, and not with the hell he'd been through before he settled down with his daughter and his life in Whiskey.

"Jesus Christ."

Loch nearly crumpled the important document in his hand before setting it down and taking a seat at the island, wondering what the hell to do next. It seemed like he was in a nightmare of responsibility and bad decisions that he couldn't wake up from, and he had a feeling life wasn't through fucking with him yet. He'd left the company for Misty's sake, but he knew he would have soon anyway. Jason had been a good man, but some of the guys Loch had worked with weren't. They'd taken jobs outside of Jason's orders, had made calls Loch had never agreed with, and had done some shady things that made Loch hate the man he'd once been.

Jason had connections, high-up contacts with money, power, and lines that led directly to the tops of some governments around the world. People with the kind of power that made waves, and even more importantly, to people who dealt in shady dealings and moved *money*. Lots of money. In the upper millions—sometimes, the billions. So much money, in fact, that Loch could barely comprehend it. But Jason's connections had been good enough for the team to get into places where others couldn't and allowed them to protect the people that others thought invincible. But it was because of Jason's teams and intel that those people *were* virtually invincible. Those who didn't understand the true nature of keeping people safe and those who were on the edge of what was right would definitely want Jason's position for that kind of money. Maybe more so for that kind of power.

Loch had been a protector. Had been in security for those who needed it. But those who worked with him hadn't always seen that as an asset.

So, Loch had left.

His phone buzzed in his pocket, and he cursed, sitting up so he could dig for it again. He was surprised he hadn't broken the damn thing by sitting on it.

Ainsley: *Stop ignoring me, Loch. Please.*

He closed his eyes, wishing he had the words to say. How did he tell the woman that meant everything to him that he wasn't the right choice for her? How did he tell her that he wanted her but didn't want to fuck up their relationship more? How did he tell her that she was his everything and yet he could be nothing for her?

Loch: *We'll talk. Soon. Had a bad day. Don't want to be shitty when Misty gets here. Talk soon.*

Ainsley: *Yes. We will. And I'm sorry you had a bad day.*

Loch: *Me too.*

He put his phone away again, and when she didn't text back, he let out a sigh of relief. He had no idea what he was going to say to her, but he knew it had to be something and it had to be soon. He was hurting her with his silence, with the distance. So, as soon as he could, he'd tell her what he could. About everything.

As long as he figured out with that was first.

Chapter 5

*A*insley needed a drink, but since it was still early on a Sunday morning, people would probably frown on that. Yes, there were such things as brunch and endless mimosas, but she needed hard liquor. Bubbly champagne wasn't going to cut it.

So, of course, a dance class where she felt bloated, ugly, and fat was totally the best place for her to be.

Yay, for girl time.

Or not.

"Why do you look like you're ready to run through that window and never look back?" Kenzie asked, her voice low just in case someone came in. Though they were in the middle of a dance studio where the acoustics made that particularly difficult.

"Because I'm whiny and annoying?" Ainsley said dead-pan, blinking quickly.

Kenzie rolled her eyes. "Yes, because when I think of you, I instantly think whiny and annoying."

"Well, for all I know, that's true." Ainsley winked since she sucked at making a serious face, and Kenzie laughed.

Ainsley hadn't told Kenzie or Melody about what had happened with Loch. Everyone had been so busy and, honestly, not a lot of time had passed since the *incident*. Even if there had been time, like right at that moment for example, Ainsley wasn't sure she could tell them about it.

What could she say?

Sorry I'm acting weird, but I slept with my best friend because we were angry with each other, then got even more angry. And now we're acting strangely when we're around each other—which isn't that often. And we're not talking about anything important, and I'm so upset at him for daring to cross that line, I've been hiding behind everything and even angrier with myself for jumping over it and meeting him with the enthusiasm I did.

Oh, and I think something else is going on with him, but he's not talking about it with me. Loch might not speak often, but he's always told me everything, even if he didn't want to. That's why we're best friends.

But now I'm afraid I've lost it all.

Ainsley swallowed hard, letting her thoughts slide through her before she buried them down again so Kenzie wouldn't see them. Both of her friends were far too observant for her liking, and this wasn't the time or place to reveal her deepest secret.

At least one of them.

Getting hot and heavy and very naked with her best friend counted as one of her secrets.

A sweaty one.

"No. But, seriously, what's up with you?" Kenzie asked as they started stretching. Melody would be in the room at any moment to begin their class, and since Ainsley and Kenzie were usually the least experienced dancers in the room, it took more stretching than most to get them going. Though, today, thanks to meetings in town, an upcoming holiday, and a few colds, they were the only two students in the studio. Melody had gone to the back to use the restroom since she had to pee every ten minutes now it seemed. And since their group was small today, the class wouldn't go long. Then, they'd probably stick around for the children's dance class. Misty was taking it, and Loch would be by later to pick her up and maybe even watch her. His gym was next door after all, and Whiskey wasn't that big of a town.

That meant Ainsley couldn't avoid him forever.

Even if she weren't sure that's what she wanted to do at all.

Ainsley held back a wince and reached down to touch her toes. She wasn't out of shape since she jogged as well as worked with Loch in his gym often, but she wasn't as flexible as she used to be. She'd always been in awe and slightly jealous of those who could dance and had any sort of rhythm. She wasn't *that* bad, but she also didn't have anywhere near the level of talent some did. But like Loch's mom had said, she liked to try different things. She wanted to learn as much as she could, and she sometimes failed along the way. She was good at failing, but she was also good at picking herself up. It was something she tried to teach her students since high school chemistry wasn't the easiest thing in the world, even if she loved it.

"Ainsley?"

"Huh?"

"I asked what was wrong with you, and then you zoned out into your own world. You've been trying to reach your toes for a full two minutes now. Great pose."

Ainsley blushed, her cheeks heating as she stood up. "Sorry. I guess I'm in my head. But my back feels good from that stretch."

Kenzie raised a brow. "I guess, though knowing us, you're probably going to end up sore from that position." Then she snorted, and Ainsley rolled her eyes. "I almost said, 'that's what she said.' I have a feeling the Collins brothers have rubbed off on me."

Ainsley laughed. "Rubbed off? Should I make another joke?"

Kenzie flipped her off, and Ainsley just shook her head. "Shut up."

"Ah, my two star pupils. So much civility and grace." Melody wrapped her arms around both of their shoulders and brought the three of them together for a group hug. "Are you ready for class?"

Ainsley pulled away and put her hand on Melody's ever-growing baby bump. She hadn't been showing at all for what seemed like forever and then, overnight, she had this adorable bump that grew day by day. Pregnancy did wonderful things to people, and though Melody complained about swollen ankles and the fact that she had to hire someone to help with the studio she'd literally just opened, Ainsley knew her friend loved being pregnant.

"That's us," Ainsley said with a grin. "I'm grace."

Kenzie rolled her eyes. "I guess that makes me civility. Though, really, I should be grace compared to you, don't you think?"

"Who was it that tripped up the stairs yesterday?" Ainsley asked.

"It was because I was wearing flats," Kenzie grumbled. "If I'd worn my normal heels, it wouldn't have been a problem." The other woman normally wore stilettoes and tall wedges with her suits and cute outfits, and Ainsley had no idea how she walked in them. She even sometimes *ran* up those stairs.

"Why were you in flats?" Ainsley asked. "I could have sworn you only changed from your heels for this class."

"And thank you for that," Melody said with a laugh. "I don't know if I could handle teaching you to even stretch while in heels."

"Drag queens and strippers do it," Ainsley put in and shrugged when the others laughed. "What? It's true."

Melody held up her hands, smiling but nodding. "And they have far, *far* more talent than we could ever hope to have dancing in heels. And, yeah, ballroom dancers do it, as well, but still, let's not try out the heavy-hitting stuff until we can at least touch our toes without wincing, shall we?"

"I promise only to wear heels at work. And on dates. And in bed with Dare." Kenzie grinned like a cat in cream and shared a look with Melody.

Friends who were able to have regular sex with those they loved should have made her jealous, but Ainsley was happy for them.

Okay, so she was *mostly* happy for them. And only a little jealous.

After all, she'd just had sex this week. The best sex of her life. The roughest, hardest, sweatiest sex ever.

Seemed she was in the mood to think about sweat and sex when it came to Loch, and she wasn't sure how she felt about that.

Her inner thighs clenched involuntarily.

Apparently, she *really* liked thinking about it.

"I knew Dare had a kinky side," Melody said with a wicked grin. "I'm working on Fox's."

Ainsley almost blurted that she wanted to do the same to Loch but held herself back. First, she did *not* want to do the same to Loch. She was going to hold back when it came to him, damn it. And secondly, she hadn't told them she'd slept with Loch yet and wasn't ready for questions.

Until she talked to him.

When they figured out what they were going to do, *then* and only then would she tell her girlfriends what had happened. And she had a feeling she'd need both of them to get through what happened after.

"Anyway, if you two are done talking about sex and all your kinky goodness, we should get started on class. Am I right? Or, since it's just the three of us, should we just head to Dare's for mimosas—a virgin one for Melody, of course—and brunch?"

"Isn't a virgin mimosa just orange juice?" Melody asked, her face pulled into a pout.

"Yes, but I'm not letting my god baby have booze until she's twenty-one, call me old-fashioned." Ainsley rubbed her back, annoyed with herself for stretching as long as she had in that weird position. Maybe she really was the klutzy one of the three.

Melody rolled her eyes and rubbed her stomach at the same time. "Dork. And as much as you don't want to stay for dance class, you paid, and now I will teach. We're still in adult beginners, girls. I promise to take it easy today though and not teach anything new since I don't want to have to redo it all again next week when everyone's schedules aren't as haywire as they are."

"Sounds like a plan to me," Kenzie said, taking her position. "Before we start, has anyone heard any updates on Dennis?"

Melody shook her head even as Ainsley's stomach rolled.

"I haven't," Melody answered. "It's so scary to think that it happened so close to my studio, and right on Loch's property."

Ainsley clenched her fists, nodding. "I know,"—she paused—"it's almost as if someone *wanted* Loch involved."

"Has he said anything to you about it?" Kenzie asked.

Ainsley shook her head, not meeting her friends' eyes. He hadn't spoken to her. Not really. At least not since their night together, and as she didn't want to have to explain that, she knew she needed to move on from Loch in their conversation.

"With our schedules recently, we haven't had a lot of time to talk. But I'm sure I'll hear all about it soon."

Kenzie gave her a weird look, but Ainsley went back to stretching. "When you do, ask him if he needs anything from us, or if he knows if there will be a service for Dennis. I know Dennis didn't have any family here, but I don't know much else about him."

Ainsley nodded again. "I will. If Dennis was alone, I figure Loch will want to help. That's just who he is."

"And you'll help him too because that's who *you* are," Melody added. "I might be new to Whiskey, same as Kenzie, but we know you both."

They did, and that was the problem with Ainsley keeping secrets from them. She wasn't any good at it. Hell, she was pretty sure they both already knew that she was in love with Loch, even if it was in her own way.

"Yeah, you do. And I'll let you know what he says. Now, ready to dance?"

"Isn't that my line?" Melody winked. "Okay, girls. Let's do it!"

Ainsley's muscles already ached.

"WATCHING these little kids dance reminds me that my body doesn't stretch that way anymore," Kenzie whispered from her seat on the floor next to Ainsley. They had finished their class the hour before and now sat watching the next class, the little beginners. Kenzie's future stepson Nate was in the class, as was Misty. Nate's mom couldn't make it thanks to a cold, but Kenzie had said she'd drop off Nate after class.

The fact that both families were making things work now after a long and drawn-out custody issue when Nate was born meant the world to Ainsley. She loved Nate like her own family and tried to be the best honorary aunt ever, just like she was with Misty.

Of course, her relationship with Misty was far different since she was in the little girl's life more than she was in Nate's, but it didn't matter, Ainsley loved those kids and watching them dance around the room and learn foot positions made Ainsley smile.

"We're old, Kenzie. Elderly, even."

Nate tripped over his feet, then righted himself as Melody worked with him on his footwork. The kid was talented and wanted to take the class because he liked Melody and wanted to hang out with Misty. And Ainsley figured he would learn balance to help him with football and other sports when he was ready to play those, as well. Nate loved all sports even at his young age, just like his dad and uncles.

"We're in our twenties, ass," Kenzie whispered. "I'm not old, just not as flexible as I used to be."

"That's not what Dare said last night," she joked.

Kenzie snorted, and Melody gave them both a look, her lips twitching before she went to help another student with her arm placement.

"Dare does appreciate what flexibility I have," her friend said dryly. "Maybe I'll try more at-home yoga or something. Because I do not want to feel this achy."

"We're just out of practice. Growing up does that."

"Too true." She paused. "Now, are you going to tell me why you keep acting weird when I mention Loch's name?" Ainsley opened her mouth to speak, but Kenzie held up her hand. "And don't tell me it's nothing. Both Melody and I know it's something."

Ainsley sighed. "We had a fight. We'll get through it." *I hope.* "But we need to talk about it first." *Soon.*

"Do you want to talk about it with me?" Kenzie's voice was low so the other parents couldn't overhear, but Ainsley still didn't want to talk about it.

"I'm okay." At Kenzie's look, Ainsley shrugged. "Really. I will be anyway. We just need to talk, and getting him to talk when he's growly isn't easy." An understatement. "And between Misty, my job, his jobs, and Dennis, things have been a little hectic."

Not to mention they were avoiding each other, but she didn't say that.

"Well, if you change your mind, I'm here. Melody, too. And now, class seems to be over and the subject of our conversation just walked in. I hope it all works out."

Ainsley hadn't needed Kenzie to tell her that Loch was

near. Her body had told her as much, and she hated that little alarm system of hers.

She stood up with Kenzie, and they both grabbed their jackets along the way. Ainsley immediately went to Loch's side while Kenzie went over to talk to the mom of the other boy in class. Ainsley hoped both boys would stay enrolled. Dancing was good for the soul, at least that's what Melody taught, and Ainsley figured it had to be true given how much it had healed Melody over the years.

Ainsley found herself standing beside Loch, aware that a few moms were whispering like usual when it came to the two of them. Many people in Whiskey figured she and Loch were having an affair behind closed doors, little did they know that the first time she'd touched him like she'd wanted to in her dreams had been only a few days prior.

"Hey," Ainsley said, trying to keep her voice positive and upbeat. She was so damn tired of feeling weird, so damn angry that he'd kissed her and yet upset it hadn't happened before that night. To say she was confused would be an understatement of epic proportions.

"Hey. Class over? Sorry I missed most of it. I couldn't get away from the gym like I wanted. Phone calls and crap."

She frowned at him, noticing the lines at the corners of his eyes and mouth. Something was wrong, and she didn't think it had to do with her—at least not entirely. And as much as she wanted to ask him about it, this wasn't the place to talk about anything important.

"Anything I can do to help?"

He didn't meet her gaze, just shook his head. "You do too much already."

She didn't like his tone, the way he sounded almost defeated, so she frowned. "What do you mean by that?"

Loch didn't have time to answer her as Misty ran up to them at that moment, her jacket already on, bouncing on her feet.

"Dad! You're here. I can't wait for our reci—rei—"

"Recital," Ainsley and Loch helped at the same time, and she forced herself not to look at him and smile.

She hated things being so weird.

"Yeah, that. I can't wait. You're going to love it. Ainsley! All the other moms are going to talk about costumes. I can't wait!"

She bounced and twirled around them both before taking Loch's hand and tugging him toward the door.

"Ice cream! It's after dance class, and that means ice cream!" Misty's voice apparently only had one level today, but Ainsley could only hear every other word or so.

Other moms.

Misty had said *other* moms.

As in, Ainsley being one of them.

Her stomach clenched, and her hands started shaking, her skin practically breaking out into a sweat. She looked up into Loch's eyes, hoping to hell she'd see something there that would make sense, that would help her figure out what to say. Only, she didn't see anything.

Just coldness.

Darkness.

Blankness.

"Ainsley! Dad! We need to go!"

Misty tugged on both of them and, somehow, Ainsley found herself outside with Loch, alone on the street since everyone else seemingly had somewhere else to be or were on Main Street shopping or eating.

"Ice cream sounds good," she said, her voice a bit wooden. "What do you say?"

Loch didn't say anything. Instead, he turned and walked toward the corner of the street, Misty's hand in his. Ainsley followed, wondering what the hell she was going to do. It was just a slip of the tongue, Misty calling her Mom —even indirectly. It was an accident. Misty was young and still learning how everything worked.

And maybe Ainsley was the only one who'd had a reaction to the word at all. Maybe it was only her that was freaking out. Maybe Loch didn't care. Maybe he didn't look blank, or dark, or cold at all and she was imagining it.

Maybe it was all just Ainsley.

She hoped to hell and back that was the truth, but as Misty talked a mile a minute while eating the ice cream they'd purchased a minute ago, and Loch walked without saying a word with Ainsley following, she wasn't really sure. They walked into the house, taking off their coats while Misty still rambled about class. That kid could talk for hours, and Ainsley had always found it cute. Right then, she thought it a lifeline.

"Misty," Loch said quickly, his daughter quickly

quieting down. "Go eat your ice cream in your room for a bit, okay? I need to talk with Ainsley."

Misty frowned, and Ainsley swallowed hard, trying to smile and not look like she was worried at all. "But I'm not allowed to eat in my room."

"Just a special thing today. Okay, baby?"

She nodded, and Ainsley reached out to instinctively hand over a couple of paper towels. Loch met her gaze, then ran his hand over his little girl's head before turning to Ainsley.

"Loch."

"This isn't working out, Ainsley."

She froze, her heart in her throat. She swore the thudding in her ears had intensified to the point where she couldn't hear correctly. She couldn't have heard correctly.

"What?" she croaked.

"This. All of this. You, me, Misty. It's confusing her. You heard her in there. She doesn't know what to call you and, fuck it, Ainsley, I've been relying on you far too much. I have since she was born, and that's not fair to any of us. It's really not fair to you. It would be better if you weren't here. If you weren't…part of everything and confusing her."

"I'm your friend. It's what friends do." Why was she breaking inside? Why did this hurt so much?

He shook his head. "You've done everything a mom does for that girl, and you never asked for a thing. You're putting your whole life on hold for her…for me, and I can't ask you to do that anymore."

Even as Ainsley broke, rage swirled inside her, causing her hand to shake. "You never asked. I gave."

"And I never gave anything back."

"I never asked you to. You always helped me, Loch. We're friends. That's what friends do."

"And then we slept together and fucked it all up. Now it's confusing, and Misty is just going to get older and be more confused." He shook his head. "I'm going to find a babysitter or a nanny or something. Someone who has clear lines where I won't hurt anyone when the lines get as blurred as they are. I should have done this earlier, but I relied on you too much. You need to go out and have a life, Ainsley. You need to be with someone who can give you something. That's not me. Okay? I'm not safe. I'm not a safe bet. And having you in my daughter's life as you are is just going to hurt you both in the end. I can't do that. I can't hurt her, Ainsley." He paused, and Ainsley blinked away tears. "And I can't hurt you."

She licked her lips, trying to understand what was going on. What exactly could she say? There wasn't anything for her to do or say. So much had been packed into that statement, it would take Ainsley hours to untangle it all, and she didn't know if she had hours to give, not when she felt like she was dying inside.

"You already did," she whispered, her voice hollow. "You already hurt me. I'm going to go. Again. Because I need to think. But don't you *dare* tell that little girl anything. If you've ever cared for me, you won't change anything.

Not yet. But…but I'm leaving. Because it hurts to look at you right now. It hurts to be near you."

It hurts to love you.

He didn't say anything as she made her way out of the house, not even saying goodbye to the two people she loved most in the world. When she closed the door behind her, she let the cold wind cool down her face, her tears finally free to fall.

She had no idea what she was going to do next. What she was going to say.

All she knew was that her world had tipped off its axis and she was now tumbling down into the abyss.

And, somehow…somehow, she had to find her way out of it.

At least, she hoped she could.

Chapter 6

*L*och was an asshole. He knew that, but he couldn't change it. But as he tried to get through the day, sipping his afternoon coffee, he knew he'd never be able to figure out how that conversation could have gone better.

He'd known he needed to push Ainsley away to keep her safe—from himself and from what might be on the horizon—but he hadn't known it would hurt so badly. He'd done it because of the company and what might be coming for Loch responsibility and past-wise. Being with him wasn't safe. He'd always known that, but now that he'd pushed Ainsley away, he was afraid he'd broken something. Irrevocably.

He'd never be able to get that look on her face out of his head. The one after he'd said the words he hadn't wanted to say. But he'd known he needed to speak them.

Then she'd left, telling him she would be back to talk. He knew she would come, too, because that was Ainsley. She never backed down from anything. Always came at things from a logical if somewhat emotional place. It sounded like a contradiction, but it was all Ainsley.

He'd hurt her, he knew that, but he hadn't known what else to do. They'd somehow woven themselves into each other's lives so completely and had become so tangled that he wasn't sure how to make sure he didn't hurt her any more than he already had. Except to push her away. A clean break, a cut that could heal rather than a jagged scar that would never do so. If he let her stay in his life just as his friend, it would be torture for both of them.

Or at least for him.

He wanted her. He *needed* her. And if he actually thought about his feelings rather than burying them away like he'd been forced to do when he found out that he was going to be a father in a world where he didn't have answers, then he'd realize he was drowning in a sea of what-ifs he couldn't hold onto.

It wasn't safe being with him. It never had been. Marnie had seen that. She hadn't loved him, hadn't wanted him except for the little money he could provide and a lot of sex. When she'd found out that she was pregnant, she'd freaked out and almost aborted Misty before Loch had even known they were having a baby.

She'd changed her mind at the last moment, and Loch had never been more grateful. Yeah, Marnie had signed over full custody and left Whiskey without a second glance, but he'd gotten Misty out of the deal.

And Ainsley had come with it, too. She'd been in his life for longer than the friendship they shared. He'd always known who she was, because she'd known his younger sister, Tabby. He'd thought her a pretty decent person who he'd let be in Tabby's life because he was the overprotective brother that didn't want his little sister hurt. And then Ainsley had grown up and stayed in Whiskey. And they'd become friends.

Best friends.

He wasn't sure how it had happened, but one day, they were having coffee, talking about school for her and work for him; and the next, she was staying over on the couch because they'd had too much to drink. Sure, she'd been underage, and he probably shouldn't have bought the beer, but he'd been an idiot. The next morning, they hadn't looked at each other like they were crazy but had instead carried on a conversation as if sleeping over at a friend's house were nothing.

They clicked. They meshed. They did all of that.

She knew almost every part of him, held nearly every memory within her.

He'd even told her about some of his past with the company, the things he'd been allowed to say anyway. He might not work for them anymore, but he'd always kept the secrets he needed to for himself and his clients.

And now he owned the company.

Loch leaned against the kitchen counter, cradling his

coffee mug in his hands as he tried to get his head on straight.

How the hell had this happened?

Why the *fuck* had Jason given him the company? The man had known Loch didn't want anything to do with the place after he left. Marnie getting pregnant had been the final straw, but he'd been well on his way out of the company long before that. He'd been working on setting up his gym, and because he'd needed the money to make that happen, he'd also set up his security system business on the side. He'd done all of that while still taking the occasional job for Jason, being a bodyguard for some celebrity who hadn't really needed him, or being extra security for clients he didn't know the name of because he hadn't been granted that level of clearance.

He'd never been a mercenary, contrary to what his brothers and sister might have thought at one point when they'd made offhand comments about it.

Riker and some of the other guys in the company might have been, though. And that had always worried Loch.

Riker worried Loch.

The man had been his second and was an arrogant asshole. Riker hated following orders that weren't his own or didn't come directly from Jason. It seemed he felt like he was next in line for whatever was coming next for the company.

Loch hadn't heard from the other man since he'd quit the company and decided to stay in Whiskey instead of just making it his home base like before. And that worried him.

Why hadn't the other man contacted him when Jason died?

Loch had done a quick search and had found a short obituary stating that Jason had died of natural causes. With no family, the other man had been put to rest by friends.

Jason had been a stern taskmaster and boss, as well as Loch's mentor, but he hadn't been someone Loch would call a friend. Not really. They were friend*ly* but they weren't *friends*, not in the sense of the word Loch had learned over the years with Ainsley and his brothers and sister. Yes, Jason had helped Loch get his head on straight and later let him talk some things out, but there had always been a sense that Jason was just a little older, a little more like a father figure.

So, who had buried him? The company? If that were the case, then why hadn't any of them contacted Loch?

And why did Loch hear about now owning the damn company—at least in the preliminary papers—from a damn lawyer who hadn't even bothered to call?

It didn't make any sense.

Riker had been Jason's second once Loch left, and that meant that Riker should have been the one to get the company. Either that, or the whole thing should have been dissolved. That's what Loch planned to do if he could now. Because he wanted nothing to do with the company, and he didn't think he could trust any of the guys he'd left behind to make sure the place didn't go to the dark side. The company had the kind of connections and reputation where they could go into any government or high-ranking official's office and work it from the inside. If you had a moral code, then protection was the key. If you didn't? Then the cost could be staggering—losses of money *and* life.

And that was just another reason why Loch couldn't get Dennis out of his mind.

It just seemed far too coincidental in Loch's mind that a man close to him—at least in proximity and profession—should be murdered on his property right about the time when Loch found out that he was now the new owner of the company—and Riker had been suspiciously silent about it all.

There was nothing silent about Riker, not unless the man was coming at someone from behind.

A quiet Riker was a deadly and dangerous Riker.

And then there was that ominous note.

Maybe Loch was losing his mind and connecting the things when they really didn't need to be connected, but it wasn't until *after* he'd spoken with the cops and saw the documents that he'd started thinking. It wasn't as if he could go to the local detectives and tell them that he hadn't heard from a man he used to know in a while so maybe he was connected to Dennis's death. It made no sense, and it probably wasn't even true, but since Loch couldn't shake it, he kept thinking about it.

And he'd keep turning it over in his mind until he

made sense of it all. Loch's brain was a Rubik's Cube sometimes, and he'd find a way to discover the right pattern.

But until he did, Loch needed to keep those he cared about safe.

That meant that Ainsley needed to stay away. Not just because of his imaginary worry about Riker, but because he was afraid if he kept her near, he might just fall for her. And that wouldn't be good for either of them. He'd break her heart, shatter his daughter's heart, and ruin it all. So, the more distance they kept between them, the better.

Even thinking those thoughts made him feel like he was doing the wrong thing and overthinking everything. So, he pushed those ideas out of his head and told himself that he'd made the right decision.

The other person he needed to keep safe was currently walking into the kitchen, a scowl on her sweet face.

"I don't want to go to other grandma and grandpa's," Misty pouted. "I want to stay home and watch a movie with Ainsley."

Loch pinched the bridge of his nose after setting down his coffee. "We already went over this, Misty. This week, you're staying with your grandma and grandpa while Ainsley works at her house." He paused, looking up and across the kitchen so he could see Misty's face. "And stop calling them other grandpa and grandma. You know that hurts them."

Misty sighed, a little more dramatic than usual, and he knew she'd only get more so as the conversation wore on.

And, hell, as she got older. She was so much like his sister Tabby sometimes, it was scary.

Well, a mix of Tabby and Ainsley, but Loch tried hard not to think of that. Attempted to ignore the fact that, sometimes, he only saw a little bit of Marnie in her; and, at other times, nothing at all.

"I don't want to hurt them," Misty muttered. "But I don't want to stay with them. Why do I have to?"

Loch went over to her and knelt in front of her. His little girl was getting so big that it was sometimes startling how she could meet his eyes when he was down on the ground. He used to be able to hold her in one arm, her little head in his big hand as he did his best not to break the greatest miracle of his life.

"Because you love them, and they love you. And you spend a night or two at their house every two months because it's a big slumber party for you."

Loch hadn't always been a fan of the arrangement, and it wasn't part of the custody agreement. In fact, Marnie's parents didn't have a single right to see their daughter's daughter. Loch's mother, however, had sat down with him right when Marnie left, and he'd felt like he was alone.

"Loch, son, you need to make sure that little girl has as much family as she can," she had said. "I know Marnie is gone. And while I'll never forgive her for doing that to this perfect baby girl, I will say, I'm glad she left." She'd held up her hand when he looked at her as if she were insane. "You don't have to fight for custody. This little girl doesn't have to grow up knowing a woman who would one day leave her anyway. Instead, she'll never know Marnie. That woman gave the little girl her DNA and her name, but that's it. But, Marnie's parents? They are trying, Loch. They saw their daughter fail and push them out of her life. They have nothing else. But I know people, and I know they will do well by that baby girl. I'm not saying open your doors to them at all hours but allow them to help. Allow them to know their granddaughter. I love this little girl with all my heart already, and I've only known her for a few hours. Let them have that, too. As much as it pains me to share her with anyone because I'm selfish that way." She'd winked, and he'd fallen in love with his mother all over again. She was so damn strong, so damn caring. And she never backed down.

So, he'd gone to Marnie's parents after Misty was born and had tried to find a solution to the problem. At first, it had been visitation at his house, but he'd never been a fan of people in his home—the fact that Ainsley had always been a part of it had been a surprise in and of itself. He also hadn't liked the idea that he was basically supervising their visits. He'd gotten to know the older couple over the past four years, and he knew they'd do anything to keep Misty happy and safe.

So, he'd installed the best security he had at their house, even better than what he had at his own because their place had fewer blind spots thanks to architecture. They hadn't given him weird looks about his hypersensitivity when it came to safety and had even welcomed it.

Marnie's parents and Misty had had dinners together without Loch. And, at first, he'd been a grumpy asshole about it because he missed his kid. Then, he'd gotten over himself because Misty had come to like it.

The whole week at the grandparents' thing was new and had only happened once before because Loch had been forced to go out of town. But he'd called last night and asked if it could happen again. The couple hadn't asked questions, they just wanted to spend time with their granddaughter.

And Loch needed his kid to be safe.

Between school and being at her grandparents' house, Misty would be safe and sound and not near him in case this whole Riker thing wasn't just in his mind. He figured a week would be long enough for him to find out. And if he were being paranoid, then Misty had a whole week with people who loved her, and he would get peace of mind.

He wasn't the world's most normal father, but he, like his brothers joked, had a special set of skills and knew how to use them.

Jesus, I need more sleep if I'm quoting Liam Neeson.

"I want to stay with Ainsley," Misty whined, and Loch knew trying to keep any form of distance between Ainsley and Misty might be far harder than he'd thought.

He didn't want Misty to be confused. Didn't want her to think of Ainsley as her mom as she had at the dance studio. Hell, he didn't want her to think that Ainsley would always be there. What would happen when Ainsley found the man of her dreams and had children of her own?

Of course, for that to happen, the man would have to live because Loch just might kill the bastard for daring to touch what was his.

And that was enough of that because, fuck it, she wasn't his. Hadn't he just proven that when he pushed her away because he was an asshole?

An asshole who got way too fucking scared when shit got real when it came to her, so he wasn't going to let things get real.

"I know you want Ainsley, but she has to work, and you need to stay with your grandparents. You love them, and they love you," he repeated. He wanted to say it to himself again because he was literally shipping off his kid so he could make sure she was safe.

And not really telling anyone about it because he really didn't know if he believed the connections with the whole Riker and Dennis and the company thing.

He just needed to figure out where Riker was, let the authorities figure out who killed Dennis, and hope to hell and back that the two weren't connected.

"She can work here. Or with Grandma and Grandpa."

"I said no. Ainsley has her own life. She's not part of ours all the time, Misty. We need to let her be." He didn't make his voice hard or even forceful, but he had to make sure Misty understood. He just had no idea how to explain it all to a four-year-old.

He didn't understand it completely himself.

"I hate you." She narrowed her eyes at him, and some part of him broke. He'd suspected words like this were coming. Kids learned them from others and thought that was how they should lash out. Misty didn't mean it since she didn't really understand the words.

It didn't make it any easier for Loch to hear.

She was his blood, his future, and he knew it would only get worse and yet sweeter as she grew older. This was parenting.

And it sucked balls.

"You don't hate me. You're four. No TV tonight when I drop you off just for that."

She opened her mouth to say something else, and he leaned forward and kissed her nose.

"I love you, Misty Collins. You're my baby girl. But you don't get to use words like *hate* until you know what they really mean. And you don't get to know what they really mean until you're older."

It was as good as he could put it. When she actually got older, he'd have to find ways to make her understand, hell, to make himself understand. But, for now, he just hoped he knew what he was doing.

Just like any dad.

Tears welled in Misty's eyes, and he hugged her close. "Love you," he repeated, kissing the top of her head.

"I love you, too, Daddy. I don't hate you. I just love Ainsley, too."

He closed his eyes and just kept hugging his baby girl.

This is the problem, he thought. Loving Ainsley was at the center of it all.

BY THE TIME he dropped Misty off at her grandparents' with all her things and reassurances that he'd video chat with her every night and afternoon plus call her grandparents for updates, he was tired. But he knew that his evening was only beginning.

Marnie's parents had been full of questioning gazes, and he'd only explained that there might be stuff from his old job getting in the way. They knew he'd been in security, and since he'd told them that he'd never killed a person and had always been on the right side of the law, they believed him. They also knew that, sometimes, even being on the right side made you enemies of those on the wrong one.

So, they'd promised to entertain inside and keep the security system on lockdown. It was the best Loch could do, and he really hoped he was just overreacting. Knowing him, he probably was, but he could never be too careful when it came to his daughter's life. If what he thought might be happening actually *was*, they'd come to his house. They'd come to *him*. And both Misty and Ainsley would be out of the way when they did.

Or…he was fucking losing his mind.

If he were overreacting, then his kid had a week with her grandparents like she'd wanted to do before she changed her mind because she was in a bad mood. She'd have time with people he knew she needed to get to know more because they loved her—even if her mother hadn't. Misty had been dealt the worst of blows when it came to mothers, but Marnie's parents were good people. And

Loch had to remember that, even if he hated that his daughter knew she hadn't been wanted by the one person who should have loved her no matter what. No amount of love from others could change that, no matter how hard he tried to make it so.

While he really wanted a glass of whiskey, Loch opened a bottle of fizzy water that Ainsley had left at his house since he desired the carbonation but not the caffeine. Then he started looking over his papers, trying to figure out what to do with the company he wanted nothing to do with.

The knock on the door surprised him, making him almost completely knock his drink over onto his papers. He shook his head, cleaned up the small spill that made it to the table and went to open the front door after looking through the peephole.

"Ainsley." He didn't sigh as he said it, and ignored the clutch in his gut at the sight of her. She was so damn beautiful, a fact he'd forced himself to ignore the entire time he'd known her. At least until the other night. How was he supposed to keep her away when she kept coming back?

"Loch." She raised her chin. "We need to talk."

And the hell of it was, he figured they did.

Even if it hurt.

Chapter 7

*A*insley had pretty much used up most of her courage walking up to the door and looking Loch right in the eyes. She hoped she'd figure out how to gain some more soon.

As in, right now.

Loch moved to the side, and she held up her chin, stepping into his home like she was welcome and not like she'd been practically kicked out the last time she was here. When he closed the door behind them both, she turned, trying not to look at him too closely.

That was the problem when it came to Loch Collins. She always looked, always wanted to see beneath the surface.

And the surface was damn pretty.

She loved his strong jawline, the fact that the line tensed up and revealed little divots at the top when he got angry or thoughtful. He didn't have dimples, but then again, he rarely smiled unless it came to Misty. He'd recently let his hair grow slightly, just long enough that Ainsley could slide her fingers through it if she wanted to. Long enough that she *had* slid her fingers through it when he'd slipped into her.

She swallowed hard, pushing those thoughts back, though those memories were one of the reasons she was here in front of him.

He wore a button-down shirt and jeans, and she couldn't help but look at the skin peeking out at his neckline since he'd left the top button undone. Then her gaze traveled down his body, his broad shoulders, the waist she knew was all muscle, the core capable of helping him lift her up when he was inside her so they could find a new position. His thighs were thick and stretched the fabric of his jeans. She knew he was hard muscle and strength all over, and knew *exactly* what to do with every inch of him.

And she did mean *every* inch.

His feet were bare, something he often did in the house. Before Misty, when he'd been working for his old job, he always had his shoes on as if he had one foot out the door and into danger at all times. When Misty was born, and he'd settled fully in Whiskey, she'd noticed that he had taken to going barefoot in the house, having others take off their shoes at the door when they stopped by, as well.

The gesture made the house a home, his life one of family rather than a journey through whatever hell he'd been in before.

Ainsley didn't know why she studied him like this, why she wanted to know more about him. He'd pushed her away, and she knew it had to be because of fear. Of what, she didn't know, but she was going to find out.

She cared about that little girl and the man in front of her far too much to back down when her feelings ended up hurt.

"I can't believe you said the words you did the last time I was here." She did her best not to let the pain she felt slide into her words, but since this was Loch and he knew every part of her—except the parts she hid deep down and kept from the world—she wasn't sure she succeeded.

"Ainsley."

She held up her hand, thankful that he shut up when she did. "No, you had your turn to talk last time. Now, it's my turn."

He swallowed hard, and she watched the way his throat worked.

Damn him.

But she still wasn't going to back down.

Not now.

And maybe not ever.

She deserved more.

She deserved answers.

"What you said before, hurt me. It was wrong and completely out of the blue. I don't know why you think you can just push me out of the way after…however many years we've stood side by side. But, Loch? It doesn't work that way. Friendships like we have don't just end because someone had a bad day. And, yeah, a bad day might not be the right way to put it, but since you're not telling me a single *fucking* thing, then that's all I have to go on."

Her chest ached, and she took a deep breath, trying to collect her thoughts. She'd almost written out a plan, an actual speech, but had decided that would be way too analytical for her when her feelings for Loch were anything but. There was no way she could put what they had together, what she thought they *could* have if they only gave it a chance, or what they could *lose* in a neat and tidy list.

A list would have made what she was going through right then easier, however.

"There are things I can't tell you, Ainsley. You know that. You've always known that."

She wanted to slap him.

She wanted to kiss him.

She wanted to hug him close and beg him to tell her what was wrong and why he was acting so irrationally, so...*un-Loch*.

"I know you had this mysterious job where you saved the world. I know you weren't a Teen Titan or Batman." She paused. "Well, I assume you aren't Batman or Captain America, but what do I know."

"You're mixing up DC and Marvel, Ainsley."

She closed her eyes, counted to five. "Not the point. What I'm saying is, no matter the cape or the mask you think you wear or used to wear, you aren't that person. Are you telling me that you're acting the way you are because of your old job? Because of your mysterious past that might make you all dark and sexy to others but always worried me because you never talk about it?"

She hadn't meant to mention that last part but, hell, she was opening herself, baring her soul in more ways than one. She'd already bared everything else on his couch, why not this?

He pinched the bridge of his nose. "Ainsley."

Whenever he said her name like that, it was because she was getting on his nerves—something she'd apparently been doing more than usual lately. Well, tough cookies, because he was pissing her off.

"Don't *Ainsley* me." She deliberately mocked the tone of his voice, and he raised a brow. How he could raise one brow independently of the other always fascinated her. But that was off-topic. Again. "Why are you pushing me away, Loch?" She swallowed hard, ignoring the pain that statement brought. "Things were working out."

"We fucked, and we fucked up."

She narrowed her eyes at the lack of emotion in his voice. "Don't. Don't try to call what we did just fucking. Yes, we got angry with each other, and something happened. But it wasn't just fucking. If it had been, then we'd be able to talk about it like adults rather than hiding from each other. Something we never do. You're my best friend, Loch. I don't get why you're acting this way."

She met his gaze, forcing herself to continue before he could get a word in and break her heart irrevocably.

"Why are you pushing me away?" she asked again. "Why are you hurting that little girl?" At the flare in his eyes, Ainsley continued. "Because you are, and you know it. She called me Mom in passing and not even directly, and we both know it probably happened before, and we just didn't notice. We knew it *could* happen. Hell, she could call Kenzie or Melody 'Mom' by accident. She's *four*. She sees other children with women in their lives and sometimes the word sticks. I know I'm not Misty's mom." Once again, she ignored the pain in her chest at that thought. She *wasn't* Misty's mom, but she was damn close—even if Loch never wanted her to be. "I love that little girl with everything I have. I held her when she was so tiny we both thought we'd break her. I was there for her first steps when she went straight to you because she loves your smile." A smile Ainsley hadn't seen enough of these days. "I was there when she went to her first day of preschool. I was there when we tried to bake cookies for the first time and almost burned down your kitchen." She let out a breath. "I was *there*."

"And that confused her…"

"Shut up." Ainsley held up her hand again. "No, just shut up. It might have been a little confusing, but not once did you treat me like I was your wife, your girlfriend, or anything other than your friend. I have been a constant in Misty's life and, hell, a constant in yours, too. If sleeping with me changed all of that, then we need to talk about it."

"It was a mistake, Ainsley." Loch whispered the words, but he may as well have shouted them.

She raised her chin, telling herself if she cried right then she'd hate herself forever. "That we slept together?

Fine. But don't take it out on Misty. Don't take her away from me." She paused. "Don't take yourself away from me either."

She whispered the last part, and he took a step toward her. For some reason, she didn't back away like she should have.

When he cupped her face, she didn't close her eyes, didn't lean into his touch. He was so warm, so big, and yet…and yet there was something inside each of them that wasn't warm, something that could break them both. And because of that, she was so scared she could hardly catch her breath.

"I'm not taking anything out on Misty. I'm thinking of her. She's the first person I think of. The only person I need to be thinking of."

That shouldn't hurt because, damn it, Loch was an amazing father and always put Misty first, but the fact that he'd said the word *only* hurt more than it should.

"She should always come first. But why can't I be on that list?" Damn it. She was begging. She heard herself and didn't like the words coming out of her mouth. Didn't like how she sounded. But she couldn't stop digging and trying to understand what was going on with him.

He was hiding something. Ainsley knew enough about him to see that he was keeping something buried. Loch was pushing her away, keeping Misty away from him, as well… but Ainsley couldn't figure out why.

He'd mentioned his past, his old job, and the secrets he needed to keep. How was it all connected? Ainsley hated being out of the loop, hated mysteries, but she needed to know why he was pushing her away.

"We shouldn't have slept together. It was a momentary lapse in judgment. It shifted something with us, changed everything. And I can't let that happen. Don't you see that, Ainsley? I can't let a mistake I made hurt my daughter." He paused. "I can't let a mistake hurt you."

She narrowed her eyes, hearing the lies. "Don't call it a mistake. Because, fuck you, Loch Collins. You were the one stripping me. You were the one sinking that dick of yours into me over and over again. Yeah, I'm using the dirty words, so you can get that self-righteous look right off your face. I don't understand you right now. You're going in circles even more than I am."

She blew out a breath, annoyed as hell that he wasn't making any sense and it was making her sound like she was crazy.

"You want it straight? I told you before, we need to give each other space."

"And I'm telling *you* that you're lying to me. You're many things, Loch, but you aren't a liar. You were the one who kissed me, remember? You were the one who said you *saw* me. That you couldn't *stop* seeing me. So, what's going on with you? You're the one who kissed me first, the one who *wanted* to kiss me. So why are you now changing your mind?"

A sudden, terrible thought slid through her, and she hoped to hell she was wrong. Because if she weren't, she might be sick.

"Was I...was it not what you wanted? Is that why you're pushing me away? Why you're lying about everything? Because I can tell when you lie to me, Loch. And you're definitely not telling me the whole truth about everything we've discussed today."

Loch cursed under his breath then brought her in for a tight hug, one that made her want to cry in his arms. She hated that feeling because she *hated* crying. She'd had enough to cry about when she was a kid, and she had thought she'd grown out of it.

Apparently, when it came to Loch, she hadn't.

"Jesus Christ, Ainsley." He pulled back, pinching the bridge of his nose. "I'm trying to protect you, and then you go and say shit like that."

"Protect me? From what, Loch. You're spouting crap that makes no sense. And, well...I'm not the greatest at knowing feelings and *things* when it comes to the opposite sex after...well...*sex*. I need plain words. I'm not good at subtly, which you well know."

"What happened between us? Best fucking sex of my life. Is that what you want to hear? Do you want to hear about the fact that I can't get the thought of you, the damn *taste* of you, out of my mind? It's all I can do to *not* think of you so I can focus on my damn job and my kid. There's *nothing* wrong with you, Ainsley. But the two of us have done our best to keep what we have just as friends for a reason. That reason being Misty. And, probably the fact we don't want to fuck it up."

Ainsley blew out a breath. "I know that. I've been——"

She cut herself off, not about to tell Loch that she'd been dreaming about him, wanting him for more years than she cared to admit. That she'd been falling for him and not acting on it for years was her problem, not his. But since they had each acted on what they were feeling—though exactly what he was feeling was still murky—she wasn't about to let go anytime soon. He'd called her stubborn before, but he hadn't truly seen stubborn yet. He would now.

"You've been what?"

"It doesn't matter." Not right then, anyway. "You don't want to fuck up what we have," she said, repeating his words. "Fine. But we slept together on the couch that's in this room, and we're both pointedly not looking at it. We need to talk about what's next, and you saying you want me out of your life completely isn't the answer. I'm not accepting that. If you want to go back to being best friends, and not talk about what we did together after tonight... fine." Not fine, but she'd deal. She had before. "But don't use Misty as an excuse. Okay? You're better than that."

He growled low, then turned away from her, his hands fisted at his sides. "There are things you don't know."

"Then tell me, damn it. Tell me if you're going to use it against me. I deserve that much."

He still didn't turn around.

"You deserve more than me, Ainsley. You always did."

For some reason, his words didn't affect her, didn't make her feel cherished or cared for. Instead, they just pissed her off even more.

"Seriously? That's the line you're going to use. I *know* you, Loch. I also know who I am and what I do or do not deserve. Once again, you don't get to take that away from me. You don't get to make my choices for me."

"And you get to make mine?" he asked, turning to look at her.

She tried not to look into his eyes because, if she did, she knew she'd break. She didn't have time for that. "That's not what I'm saying. I'm not making your choices. I never have, and you know damn well I wouldn't be able to. But I don't understand what's going on. Why isn't Misty here? Why are you pushing me away? What's going on with you? Why are you so quiet about Dennis? About… everything? And why don't you want to talk about what happened between us?"

Loch was saved from having to answer any of her questions by a knock at the door. Ainsley had never been so angry or relieved to hear it.

Because if Loch were to tell her to leave again, she would. She couldn't be a woman who begged. Not anymore, or more than she already had. But she couldn't let their friendship die. She needed to fight for it. Only she wasn't sure how. Not anymore.

Not when she was breaking inside.

Chapter 8

*L*och's skin itched, and it was all he could do to keep from pulling Ainsley into his arms. He wanted to hold her, be with her, have her as his. He wanted to take her and Misty away from all of this crap. He'd done his best to never think about Ainsley in any way but as his friend, but now he couldn't help but think of every glance and touch they'd ever shared.

But he couldn't do anything about it.

Not with Riker in the wind, a murderer in Whiskey, and a possible connection between the two that could have disastrous consequences for everyone near him.

Loch passed Ainsley so he could get to the front door, his jaw clenching when he saw both of his brothers through the peephole.

"What do they want?" he mumbled.

"Who?" Ainsley asked from behind him. "And why are you *armed*?"

Shit. Loch had forgotten he had his gun on him. He had a concealed carry permit, and since Misty wasn't in the house, he was wearing the gun. But, still, Ainsley didn't need to see that shit.

"I need to put it in the safe. Just got back from the gun range." A lie, but he didn't look at her to see if she believed him. Instead, he opened the door, growling as Dare and Fox pushed past him, intense looks on their faces.

Apparently, today was the day to confront Loch. Too bad no one had told him about it.

"Loch," Fox said with a raised brow as he slid past. "Ainsley."

"Fox. Dare."

"Ainsley."

Loch closed the door behind them, locking it and throwing the deadbolt. He quickly put in his security code before the alarm went off and turned to glare at the people in his house. Those who needed to be far away from him while he figured all of this shit out. Loch's hands still threatened to shake from his conversation with Ainsley. He'd known she would be at his doorstep soon, he just hadn't planned on having her there tonight. He'd needed more time to figure out what to say to her, what he *could* say to her. And because he hadn't been ready when she showed up—something very unlike him—he'd gone in circles just like she'd said. He'd lied, he'd said the wrong things more than once, and they still hadn't gotten anywhere with what they needed to discuss.

And now he knew that he and Ainsley would end their night on the side of a virtual jagged cliff, their conversation left undone, their relationship still in tatters. The tatters he'd been the one to create.

All because his brothers were here.

Staring.

"You guys here for a reason?" Loch's voice was a rough growl, and he didn't really care. Whatever was making him edgy felt as if it were getting closer and, frankly, he needed to talk to Ainsley, not to the two other men in the room.

"You're always so welcoming," Dare drawled, glancing between him and Ainsley. "We interrupting something?"

"No," Loch and Ainsley said at the same time, the tone biting.

Dare's brows shot up, and Fox winced. "I'll take that as a yes."

"Say what you want to say since you didn't show up with a six-pack. Meaning, you're not here to relax. And I'm pretty sure you said you were working the bar tonight, Dare, so that means someone is watching it for you. And since Fox is here, too, I'm blanking on who it is."

"Dad has the bar for a bit. I was just going to work an hour tonight anyway. Dad wanted to get some hours in so he doesn't lose his touch." Dare rolled his eyes. "You know him."

Loch did, and he would bet anything that their parents were in on this, whatever *this* was. And if Dare and Fox failed in whatever they were about to do, then either Loch's parents or the guys' women would be in his face soon. He wasn't really an asshole, far from it, even though his actions lately had proven the opposite and had made him question that. But right then, he *wanted* to be the asshole, kick everyone out, and be done with it.

It wasn't going to be that easy, though. It never was.

"Okay, that explains the bar. Now, why are you here?"

"We want to know what the hell you're hiding," Dare answered. "You've always hidden things from us over the years. Your job. Marnie. All of it. I get it, I do. But something is different now, and I'm worried."

"I'd like to know, as well," Ainsley put in, and he turned to her. "What? I was asking you the same thing before, and you didn't answer. Maybe you'll tell them if you won't tell me. But we're worried about you." She looked over at his brothers and shrugged. "I'm adding myself to this since I'm here. Sorry."

Fox held up his hands. "If anyone's going to get him to talk, it's you."

"Not so sure about that," Ainsley muttered.

Before Loch could say anything about *that*, his doorbell rang, and his body tensed. "Now what?" he growled.

Dare frowned. "It's not one of us, the family. We all decided it should be me and Fox first."

Just like Loch had thought.

"Let me see who it is," Loch said on a sigh then turned on his heel to look out the peephole. When he caught sight of Detective Renkle and Detective Shannon on the other side of the door, his whole body tensed. Shit, nothing good could come of this, not when he had a feeling he knew why they were there.

"Hold onto your butts," he whispered the old line from *Jurassic Park* and one he knew his brothers and Ainsley would know, causing them to tighten ranks. Loch opened the door, rolling his shoulders back but not rising to his full height. He didn't want to look the big man, even in his own home when it came to the authorities who seemed too interested in him on this case.

"Loch? Mind if we come in?" Detective Shannon asked, his voice calm. Renkle just glared.

"What is this about?" Loch wouldn't resist, but he didn't want anyone in his home unless he knew why they were there. Because as soon as he let them into his house, who knew what might happen. He was fully aware that Riker was probably out there, most likely watching—or at least somewhere close if the letter were anything to go by. The other man had to be if he'd gone underground like Loch thought. Because even if Riker had nothing to do with the ongoing investigation with Dennis, he would want what Loch now owned. That was one thing Loch could truly be sure of.

"We can take this down to the station," Renkle added.

Since his brothers were watching and Ainsley was far too close, Loch said, "Fine with me."

Shannon shook his head. "We just have a few questions. No need to go down to the station. It *is* cold out here, though, so if we could at least come in, that would be helpful. We don't have a warrant if that's what you're worried about. This isn't that kind of visit."

Loch knew enough about procedure to let them into the house then. If things got worse, he'd have Fox call the family lawyer again, just to be careful. Loch took a step back and let them in, then met Fox's gaze. "Can you take Ainsley home?"

Fox raised a brow, but Ainsley spoke first. "I'm not going anywhere. What's going on, Loch?"

"We need to talk to Loch," Shannon said calmly. Loch figured the two detectives had talked about how to handle the situation beforehand since Renkle wasn't as loud as usual. Either that or Shannon had talked to the other man, making sure he didn't get into Loch's face too early like he had a habit of doing.

"About?" Dare asked.

Shannon sighed and looked at Loch. "We need to know where you were on the night Dennis died." The detective rattled off the exact date and timeframe, and Loch froze.

Ainsley didn't freeze, however. She moved to his side, sliding her hand into his as his brothers came in to flank him. He shouldn't have been surprised that just the feel of Ainsley next to him calmed him, or the idea that his brothers stood by his side to help. But he was shocked, just a little.

"He was with me that night. *With* me," Ainsley blurted, and Loch held back a curse. If Riker were watching the investigation, there was no way Loch would be able to push her far enough away now. No matter what he did, Riker would know that Ainsley was important to him. Though it wasn't as if he could truly get away with the lie. She was in every part of his life, just like they'd fought about before. Pushing her away had been idiotic, and just because he'd gotten scared as hell when it came to Ainsley, that didn't mean he had to keep making the wrong choices when it came to her.

Fox cursed under his breath, pulling Loch out of his thoughts. "Ainsley. You don't need to lie. He didn't do it."

Loch was truly close to thrashing his brother at that moment. Ainsley's cheeks went bright red, and he squeezed her hand, giving her a look that promised he'd kick Fox's ass later for those words. They were in front of the cops for fuck's sake, Loch would have thought his brilliant brother wouldn't keep putting his foot in his mouth. Apparently, he was wrong.

Ainsley turned on Fox. "I'm not lying. I'm not an idiot."

"She's not lying," Loch put in, aware that Shannon and Renkle were listening to everything he said. "We were together at the bar with the rest of the family during the first part of the evening, then here together, alone, until right before I showed up at the gym and talked with the authorities when I found out what happened. You don't need to know the exact details, do you? Because that's between Ainsley and me. I can give you the names of the people who saw me at the bar that night, as well as the info from my security system of when I turned it on and off when we got to my place."

"A security system you put in from a company you own," Renkle added.

Shannon glanced at his partner before looking back at Loch and Ainsley. "No details about what went on during that night after the security system was turned on are needed. But the details you said you'd offer would be helpful."

"No problem." It wasn't, but that didn't mean any of this would be easy. Riker was setting Loch up, he knew it. But he didn't know what he could legally do about it except cooperate with the police. However, telling them his theories wouldn't help, it would only make him look like a madman who didn't want a target on his back.

"Convenient timing, though," Renkle said quietly, his gaze darting between Ainsley and Loch.

"There's nothing convenient about this. And if you're done, why don't you go find out who killed Dennis, because you're not going to find that person here. Oh, and you could have asked me this before when you were talking to me, but you didn't. You didn't ask for an alibi or even touch on where I was before, so I don't know what's going on now or why you're asking all these questions, but if you need anything else from me, you can talk to my lawyer."

Shannon just nodded, while Renkle glared.

"Good to know. We'll be in touch," Shannon said. "Ainsley." The man nodded at her before doing the same to Loch's brothers and then turning to leave.

"Stay in Whiskey, Loch. You know the drill." Renkle moved out of the door first, sliding past Shannon, who let out a sigh Loch didn't think he was supposed to hear.

Loch quickly locked the door behind the two, dealing with the alarm while Dare looked out the window, watching the detectives leave.

"Renkle gives cops a bad name," his former-cop brother said with a frown. "I was never like that."

"You're not an asshole." Loch turned to look at his family, at Ainsley, and wondered what the hell had happened and why it had happened so fast. He was just glad that Misty hadn't been there to witness any of that. If she had been, he'd have found a way to keep her out of hearing range, or his brothers would have. Because there was no way Loch would let his daughter get close to this. As it was, he sent a quick text to Marnie's parents to check in, and they replied back that everything was well but that Misty might be on cake overload.

His lips quirked into a smile for an instant before the reality of the rest of the situation washed the expression from his face.

"Misty?" Ainsley asked, her voice shaky.

"Yeah. Apparently, she had too much cake."

"Not a thing," Fox put in.

"You won't think that once your kid is older," Dare said quickly. "What the hell is going on, Loch? Why are the cops questioning you like they are?"

"Because they think I have something to do with Dennis's death."

"Are they that hard up for hits?" Fox asked. "And before you say anything, this isn't going in the paper. I don't care if I'm supposed to look for breaking news, I'm not going to be the brother who puts lies in the paper just to get reads."

Loch pinched the bridge of his nose. "It honestly didn't cross my mind."

"Just making sure. Because Whiskey is a small town, and I don't like that they're questioning you like they are. It doesn't make any sense."

It did if Riker were somehow behind it. Or... "They're out of options and don't have a lead, so they're going after the guy who owns the place where the body was found and who knew the man. I had nothing to do with it, though. I was with Ainsley when it happened. They have nothing on me, and when they start looking in another direction, they'll realize that."

"They'll lay off you soon. You've done everything right. They have nothing on you. But keep with the lawyer just in case. This is the ex-cop talking," Dare said.

"It'll be fine." Loch met Ainsley's gaze, aware that she was staring at him, her eyes wide, but there was no fear there. Just anger.

That was his Ainsley.

"It'll be fine," he repeated, and she gave him a tight nod. That gesture let them both relax, at least from the way her shoulders dropped a fraction.

"So..." Fox's voice trailed off, and Loch had a feeling he wasn't going to like the words coming out of his brother's mouth. "Are we not going to talk about the whole sex thing? Because I think we should talk about the whole sex thing."

Dare cleared his throat, raising his hand. "I know we have other serious things…far, far more serious things to talk about, but I would also like to know about the whole sex thing. And I would venture to guess, so would our women."

Ainsley blushed even harder, and Loch growled.

"Get out. We'll talk tomorrow." He paused, then looked at his best friend. "Not you, Ainsley. You, stay." He needed to talk to her, but he had no idea what he was actually going to say.

His brothers shared a look but left, giving him hard hugs on their way out. No doubt they'd acquiesced so quickly because they wanted to tell their women what they'd learned—and not just about Ainsley. Loch's life was already complicated, but he had a feeling it was going to get worse.

When his brothers were gone, that left his best friend standing in front of him, her face pale, her hands shaking. "Ainsley…"

"I…I think I need…actually, I don't know what I need. Because, that…I have no idea what just happened."

He held open his arms, needing her close and not knowing what else to do. "Come here." She practically ran to him, wrapping her arms around his waist. Her warm weight was a comfort he didn't know he needed. He remembered that she was his everything, even if he didn't want her to be, at least not then, not when everything could break. "Stay." He looked down at her. "In the guest room," he clarified. "Where you usually sleep. We'll figure out the rest later. But, stay."

He needed her safe, needed her under his care until he figured out the next step. And when she nodded, his heart sped up, but his shoulders relaxed. Tonight, she would be safe. Tonight, he could think.

He'd figure out tomorrow when it came.

He hoped.

Chapter 9

---

*A*insley had settled in Loch's guest room, exhausted
yet wanting to know more. But she knew she
couldn't do anything about it. Not yet. The fact that she'd
slept there because she was scared for him and he'd looked
scared for her meant something, but she didn't know what
exactly. They hadn't talked more beyond making sure she
was ready for bed and knew where her toothbrush was.
She'd slept over countless times before while watching
Misty, and even before then when she'd slept on his couch
after a long night of movies.

It hadn't meant anything then because they were
friends, and that's what friends sometimes did. The fact
that she had a few spare changes of clothing in the guest
room, her own drawer, and her own toothbrush meant that
maybe Loch was right. Perhaps she had inserted herself
into Loch's and Misty's lives too much.

But it wasn't like she truly wanted to change that now.

She'd tossed and turned most of the night, unable to sleep with him so close with so many unanswered questions between them. She still couldn't believe everything that had happened the night before. And she was still trying to process it all: the fight, the yelling, the cops, the fact that his brothers now knew about them…

It was all a little too much, but it wasn't as if she could hide from it.

Once she was alone with Loch again, she'd find a way to calmly talk about what was going on between the two of them, as well as the important things that were happening in Whiskey. He was hiding something, she knew that. And he was holding back because he was trying to protect her. That much was clear. Loch was always trying to protect her, no matter how many times she told him she could take care of herself. She'd taken his self-defense courses—classes he'd started at the gym because he hadn't liked her walking alone at night even in their seemingly safe town. She still took them when he offered them to keep her skills fresh, and he helped her outside of them so she was always prepared.

She didn't know what exactly he feared when it came to her safety, but not only were they friends, but she also liked spending time with him for reasons she'd kept to herself for ages. She wished she knew what would have happened if his brothers hadn't shown up, or if the police hadn't come soon after.

She needed to know what Loch was hiding, and what he might have said if they'd had more time.

And she needed to know that he would be safe. Because given how she'd felt with the cops asking him questions and making it sound as if he'd been the one to kill Dennis, she didn't know if he truly was all right. It all had to be connected: his secrets, Dennis, Loch pushing her away. How, she didn't know, but she'd find a way to make him tell her. She didn't have another choice.

Ainsley sighed and parked her car in front of Melody's home, the stunning stonework making her marvel as usual. Melody had recently moved to Whiskey to stay with her grandmother, Ms. Pearl, who happened to be a fixture in the town and part of its more recent history. Fox lived there now as well, and soon, there would be a baby in the home also. Ainsley couldn't wait. She adored babies, and she loved the fact that Fox and Melody were head over heels in love with each other even more.

Tonight, Ainsley would be spending the night because the girls wanted some time with her. No doubt her friends wanted her there because their men had told them what had happened at Loch's the night before. Melody didn't mind since she needed friends to talk to about the whole situation. Friends who weren't Loch. Other women in the past hadn't understood her relationship with Loch and always tried to either hone in on it or get him for themselves. She'd never been jealous, not really, especially since she'd never been strong enough to tell him her feelings. However, she hadn't liked it when the other women dropped her as soon as Loch failed to show them any attention—or at least the attention they wanted.

Kenzie and Melody were different, and not because they'd found their futures with Loch's brothers. Ainsley had a feeling the two wouldn't have batted an eye at her friendship with Loch and wouldn't have pushed Ainsley away just to try and get closer to the man even if they had remained single.

Ainsley knew the two women had noticed her feelings for Loch, but they never pushed.

Tonight, however, there would be pushing. She knew it. And tonight, for the first time, Ainsley might be willing to open up.

She hoped.

That morning, after Melody had texted, sweetly demanding that Ainsley stay the night for girl time, Ainsley had mentioned it to Loch on their way out the door, and he'd given her a tight nod. He'd seemed happy that she wouldn't be at home alone, and since he wouldn't answer *why*, she'd rolled her eyes and left, annoyed that he was so damn protective yet wouldn't explain.

So, she would stay with Melody and Ainsley and Ms. Pearl, safe under lock and key for the night while she figured out what the hell to do next. But to do that, she needed to get out of the car and actually talk to everyone.

Melody opened the door with a wide grin, her little baby bump so adorable it was all Ainsley could do not to reach out and put her hands on it to feel her honorary niece. Ainsley held back the sudden lump in her throat at the thought.

Everyone was pairing off, moving on with their lives and becoming adults in the real sense of the word, leaving Ainsley just a little bit behind. Not that she planned to feel sorry for herself for too long about that. She had a career that she loved, and while she might not have the full-blooded siblings others might have, at least not anymore, she did have Loch and his family.

As long as she didn't lose him because of their one night together and whatever else was going on in his head.

"You can touch the bump if you want," Melody said after closing the door. "It's okay. I mean, if strangers start coming up to me and touching the bump, I might start a fight, but you're family." She winked, and that lump in Ainsley's throat tightened even more before her whole body warmed at the words.

"Yay. You're getting so big. Not that you're big, but...you know what I mean," she quickly added.

Melody snorted. "I do. Fox said something similar this morning, however, and I had to hurt him for it."

Ainsley winced. "Yeah, probably not the best thing to say to a woman who's in her second trimester." She quickly set her bag down on the floor and put her hands on the bump, sighing softly. She didn't feel a kick or even move-ment, wasn't even sure that would happen at this stage since the things she knew about pregnancy came from tele-vision and books—she taught chemistry and not biology for a reason, after all—but she still felt the connection. "You have a person growing inside you. That's so…cool."

"Cool is a word for it," Melody said with a laugh. "I'm hitting the craving period. Though, apparently, that can happen at any time during the pregnancy. I'm also starting to have to pee every ten minutes, but that could just be all in my head, knowing me."

Ainsley pulled her hand away, laughing for real for the first time since her night with Loch. She didn't want to think about that since she didn't have answers, but then again, she couldn't do much about that tonight since she and Loch would probably be the main topic of conversation with her friends. That and the investigation that set her stomach on edge.

"Maybe your mind is just getting your body prepared for when you're waddling down the hall with the baby actually pressing on your bladder."

Melody winced. "Ugh, I'm so not looking forward to that part. Plus, the whole childbirth thing scares the crap out of me, but I'll do it since I can't wait to be a mom." Her eyes shone brightly as she spoke, and Ainsley couldn't help but smile. "I know I'm going to make mistakes, and I probably won't be any good at it at first, but Grandma Pearl is already teaching me so much. Plus, Fox's mom is amazing. And I know Kenzie is learning too since she's not only in Nate's life, but I know she and Dare are ready to start trying soon, as well."

"There will be a few new Collins babies before we know it. Plus, Tabby is due soon, too."

Melody grinned. "I'm glad she's doing it first. It sort of gets the pressure off me, I guess. Though that makes me feel like a dork for saying so."

"Or maybe you're just like every other woman who is about to be a first-time mom. You're nervous and excited all at once. I can't wait to hold that baby in my arms. Just saying."

"Well, you'll be its honorary Auntie Ainsley, so expect lots of baby holding." Melody gave her a wicked grin. "Of course, from what I hear, maybe the title won't be so honorary."

Ainsley closed her eyes and groaned. "Of course, Fox told you."

"Dare told me, too," Kenzie said from behind her.

"And since I can't be left out of a secret, I know, as well," Ms. Pearl said on a laugh as she came to Ainsley's side. The older woman hugged her waist, and Melody leaned in without putting her weight on Pearl's slight frame.

"Goodie." Ainsley groaned when the others laughed, then let them lead her to the living room where assorted cheeses, dips, chips, breads, cookies, and other appetizers were laid out. The girls had gone all out, and Melody's stomach growled just looking at it all.

"Don't be like that," Kenzie said, hugging her close. "We won't talk about it if you don't want to, but it seems like a big deal."

"It *is* a big deal," Ms. Pearl added as she sank into her high-backed chair that Ainsley knew was beyond comfortable. That was Ms. Pearl, class and comfort all in one streamlined package. "But, because it's you. Because it's Loch. Not because it's a bad thing. And I would love to hear all the details because I'm not as young as I once was, and hearing the scandalous tidbits is about the only thing I get these days."

"Grandma," Melody warned, her eyes dancing with laughter.

"What? Loch is a big boy." Ms. Pearl's eyes widened in mock horror. "I mean...oh, you know what I mean."

"That was no slip of the tongue, Grandma."

"That'd better have been a slip of the tongue."

Kenzie and Ainsley fell onto the couch, holding their stomachs as they giggled like schoolgirls. Melody joined in as Ms. Pearl buffed her nails.

"I'd say my work here is done, but I don't want to leave without hearing all the dirty details." Ms. Pearl leaned forward then, her eyes cooling. "I also want to hear about what happened last night. Fox didn't say much, as I don't know what he thought he could tell us, but I've had my times dealing with law enforcement over the years, young lady. If you need me, I'm here. Same with that boy of yours."

"He's not mine, Ms. Pearl." Ainsley hadn't meant for those to be the first and only words she said. But, apparently, that was where they were going to start.

"He's yours, even if neither of you is ready to admit it."

"Grandma," Melody warned again.

Ms. Pearl held up her hands. "I'll stop for now, but why don't you start at the beginning, Ainsley. At least, the beginning of where you need to. You're practically jumping out of your skin right now, needing to let some of what you have out. We're all women here, all family. No matter what happens after tonight, what happens after this business with the law is over, you're still one of us."

Tears stung Ainsley's eyes, and Kenzie reached out and gripped her hand. She squeezed back, then leaned into Melody's shoulder. Ainsley sat on the couch between her two new friends and in front of Ms. Pearl, the woman who was already a better mother than she'd ever had, and told them about her fight with Loch.

The first fight and the lack of date that had led to their night together on this couch.

The second fight that had led to him trying to rip her out of his life.

The third fight that had ended before anything could be resolved.

The fact that there had been so many fights recently between them hurt Ainsley, but she knew there had to be a resolution soon. She just prayed it would be something she could live with.

And because she couldn't finish talking about the final fight without mentioning Fox, Dare, and the police, Ainsley told them everything she knew about the investigation and the fact that she was indeed Loch's alibi.

"I don't understand why they think Loch had anything to do with Dennis's death," Kenzie said with a frown.

"Anyone who's a local in Whiskey knew Dennis. He was a fixture at the gym and a few other places around town. I'm still pretty new here, and even I knew him."

"Same here," Melody added. "It's like the cops don't know who to pin it on, so they're looking at Loch just because he was found outside the gym. Unless there's more to it."

Ainsley shook her head. "I don't want to think like that. I want to think they are looking at all connections and will soon find the real person. There's no way it could have been Loch, and I already said I'd sign whatever I need to, even go to court or whatever happens next for alibis. I'm out of my depth on this. But, you guys, it's like Loch knows something we don't. He sent Misty away to her grandparents, and he's pushing me away to *keep me safe*. I just don't know what he thinks he's keeping me safe from."

"Then you're going to have to find out," Melody said quickly. "I can't read that man, and I haven't known him long, but I have a feeling I'm not alone in that. But if he wants to protect you from something, it's all circling around whatever is going on in Whiskey right now. It has to be important. If anyone is going to get him to talk, it's you, Ainsley."

"Easier said than done."

"Of course, it won't be easy," Ms. Pearl added. "Nothing worth fighting for is easy. I don't know that boy's past, but there's obviously something there from what he's saying. And though he wants to keep you in the dark to keep you safe, that clearly isn't working for either of you.

Explain that. Because the best way to keep yourself safe is to know what's going on around you."

"She's right," Kenzie said. "You can't let him get away with his big, bad protector role he's so good at. It took me forever to figure out what was hurting Dare, and you know my past, you know what I ran from. In the end, Dare and I knowing what each other went through helped us figure out how to get through what came after."

Ainsley gripped her friend's hand again and squeezed. Kenzie had been through hell and back. Dare too for that matter. But now the couple was getting married and thinking of adding to their family.

"I think he's going to have to tell me what's going on," Ainsley said. "I'm not going to give him another choice."

"And what about the other thing?" Kenzie asked softly. "What about you and Loch?"

Ainsley shook her head. "I don't know."

"I knew from the moment I saw you with him that you had feelings for him." Melody winced at her words. "I mean, I'm sure others didn't notice, but I was kind of on high-alert when I moved here and was thrust into your family."

Her family. They kept using those words, and Ainsley was afraid of what would happen if she and Loch didn't mend things. Would they still be her family? And what if she and Loch tried…*something*, and it went to hell?

What would she have then?

She may have loved her best friend for years, but that didn't mean she knew what to do with those emotions.

"I don't know what I'm going to do about Loch, but I do know that I'm starving, and all of this looks amazing. Can we eat and talk about silly things for a bit? We can come back to the drama that is my life later, but right now, I could use some other girl-talk."

Her friends looked at her, then at each other before everyone dug into their food and drinks. Loch was always on Ainsley's mind, even when she and the other women talked about TV shows and the latest Whiskey gossip that didn't have anything to do with mystery and death.

By the time she made it to the first-floor guest room she'd share with Kenzie for the night, she was full, exhausted, and emotionally drained. Her friend had gone back to the library for a bit to talk to Dare on the phone, and Ainsley figured she'd fall right to sleep.

She didn't count on Loch's name popping up on the screen of her phone as soon as she sat down on the bed.

She didn't want to answer.

She had to answer.

"Loch."

"Wanted to check on you." His gruff voice sent shivers down her spine, and she did her best not to moan. Because now when she heard that deep voice of his, she could only remember what he sounded like when he yelled as he came inside her.

She wouldn't be sleeping well tonight, after all.

"How's Misty?" It was the first thing she thought to ask without letting herself get angry with him or herself again.

"I talked to her earlier. She's having fun with her grandparents for the week."

"Are you going to tell me why she's there?"

"You know we planned a week with them." He didn't answer the question, not really, and they both knew it.

"Yeah, but I didn't know it was this week." Ainsley knew it had to do with whatever else was going on with him, but as long as Misty was safe and loved, Ainsley would try to understand.

"Well, it is." He cleared his throat. "Be safe tonight. I'm sorry I yelled. But there're things you don't know."

She bit her tongue so she wouldn't yell before she spoke. "I can't know them if you won't tell me." A pause. "I thought we were friends. That there weren't any secrets between us." The latter was a lie since she'd always kept her feelings from him, but it wasn't like she was on a pedestal or anything.

"We are."

"Then you aren't very good at it. Because you need to tell me. I can't stay safe like you want unless I know all the facts."

"I can't." He didn't sound as sure as he had, though. But it still hurt to hear.

"Then things will have to stay as they are, uncertain and not good for either of us." She let out a shaky breath. "Goodnight, Loch."

She hung up before he could say anything else, afraid that she'd let her tears fall. If she weren't careful, she'd lose everything. The problem was, if she didn't take a chance, she was afraid she'd realize she didn't have anything at all.

Something moved outside the window, and she froze, telling herself it was just a trick of the moonlight because she was already on edge. But, still, she went to the window, staying out of eyesight, and quickly shut the blinds before Kenzie came back.

Loch was keeping her on edge for more reasons than one, but someone *had* died in Whiskey, and the killer hadn't been caught yet. Being uneasy might just be her new state of being.

Chapter 10

*L*och's muscles strained as he finished his last chin-up, his body not showing it since he could do these in his sleep, but his mind was already exhausted from another sleepless night—not a good way to stay on top of things.

He let go of the bar, dropped to his feet, and started stretching. He was doing his best to act normal and not let anything going on around him visibly affect him. Riker had sent that note, Loch was sure of it now, and that meant that Loch couldn't be too careful when it came to anything having to do with Dennis—and now the company. His company.

Shit.

He hadn't done anything about that other than tell his lawyer. He didn't know what he was going to do, but dissolving it and walking away seemed like the best option. Yet he didn't know how to do that, especially with all the sensitive data the company dealt in, so it was just another item on the list.

After finding Riker.

Loch had sent word to his contacts to keep an eye out but not make a splash about it. He hoped to hear something soon, because things were getting a little tricky here, and Loch wanted to make sure his family was safe.

His family, including Ainsley.

He closed his eyes tight, pushing away those thoughts as he set himself up for box jumps. His gym had an open floor plan with a few rooms off to the side for classes, so as he set up his station, he could still check out the rest of the gym and who was working out.

He knew Ainsley was over on the elliptical, getting her workout in for the evening. He had known she was there since she first walked into the building. He didn't want her walking outside alone, not at night, and wasn't even comfortable with her doing it during the day, so he'd find a way to make sure she had someone with her when she went home.

But because he was a mess, he wasn't sure it would be him.

Loch rolled his neck then squared his shoulders, preparing for the jumps. He'd go slow and easy at first, get his rhythm and his balance, then increase the intensity over time. His spotter, another of his trainers, stood by, ready to help if needed. Loch may own the place and know what he was doing, but he wasn't stupid—contrary to how he felt lately.

He landed the first jump with ease, then started his counts. He was sweaty, his body aching, and almost ready to call it a day when the first whistle shot in the air. He didn't falter, but he did glare at the woman who'd done it. The woman in her sixties on the treadmill just winked, giving him a wave, and he rolled his eyes before starting the next jump.

He did it two more times, ignoring the crowd staring at him, and when he landed his final jump, one of his highest but not the highest he'd ever done, the gym erupted in cheers and applause.

His crew was laughing, and he wiped the sweat out of his eyes as some of the women in the room cat-called. He wasn't a fan of anyone doing that to *any* of the people in his gym. This was a safe place for everyone, but since the whole place had been filled with tension for the past few days after what happened with Dennis, Loch let it slide.

This time.

If it happened again, everyone would find out exactly what kind of asshole he was.

Then Loch looked up into Ainsley's face, laughter in her eyes and a smile quirking the corners of her lips, and he swallowed hard. Things weren't good between them. Hell, things were pretty damn terrible because of words spoken and decisions made. But if she could laugh, even with her eyes, and give him a small smile, then maybe it wasn't so bad.

"I'm done." He spoke to his spotter as he cleaned up, but he wasn't positive he wasn't talking to himself, as well. Because the hell of it was, when he looked at Ainsley with her darkening eyes and the sweat running down her chest as she worked out, he wasn't sure why he was staying away.

He wasn't sure why he'd ever wanted to.

And that was the problem, wasn't it? He wasn't sure of anything anymore, and it was making his thoughts tangle, and his words come out harder than he wanted. He kept making mistakes, and that could be costly when it came to whatever the hell was going on. With everything.

Riker was part of this, Loch *knew* it. He was almost positive the note had to do with him, knew the company had to be closed, and knew that whatever had happened with Dennis was only the beginning. And because it was all happening at once, Loch didn't even have time to mourn Dennis, the man he'd worked with and known in his life for long enough for it to truly matter. Or maybe, he had the time but couldn't let himself do it because if he did, he'd make more mistakes.

That's how it usually worked for him.

And if he made mistakes now, those he loved would end up getting hurt.

Including Ainsley.

Yes, Loch loved her, always had, but the idea that it could be a different kind of love wasn't something he'd allowed himself to think about for years.

Now, it was all he could think about.

He made his way to his office, closing the door behind him since he needed time to think and to work. Ainsley would be safe with so many people around, and his staff knew to come and get him when she was ready to leave. They might not understand what was going on between him and Ainsley—not like anyone did, including himself— but they knew that Loch was watching out for her. And since all of them were mourning and on edge themselves with Dennis's death, they were careful. Hell, everyone was doing such a good job of acting normally, at acting as if they weren't afraid of what was going on around them, that maybe thinking about Ainsley and Loch and what might be between them was a salve.

The door opened after a perfunctory knock, and Loch almost scowled until he looked up and saw Ainsley walk in, sweat on her brow and a guilty expression on her face. She locked the door behind her, and he figured that she didn't want anyone else to hear what she had to say.

He did his best not to notice the way her leggings cupped her ass or the fact that her sports bra pressed her tits together perfectly. Then he tried not to think about how she would look if he slid his dick between those tits of hers, and he had to quickly adjust himself behind his shorts.

Then…then, he thought about the fact that he'd already seen her naked, *felt* her naked, and wondered if maybe it was okay that he thought all those things. Because from the way her eyes darkened, he didn't think her thoughts were any purer than his.

"Hey," he said, his voice gruff. It was always gruff, but it tended to be deeper around her. He'd tried to think it was because he could be himself around her, and that was part of it, but it was more. So much more. Damn it.

"Hey." She blew out a breath. "So, I'm here to apologize."

He stood up, his eyes widening. "What the hell do you have to apologize for? I'm the one being an asshole."

Ainsley shook her head then looked him in the eyes before shrugging. "That might be the case. And it's usually the case since we're friends and we tend to be assholes to each other. I mean, if we can't trust each other to act like idiots, then what's the use?"

She was right, but before he could say anything in response, she continued. "I'm here to say I'm sorry for hanging up on you last night. It was a crap move. Yeah, you kicking me out of the house was a crap move, too, but I figured you did it because of whatever you're hiding. And when I figure that out, it'll all make sense."

He shook his head, confused as usual when it came to Ainsley. "You seem pretty confident that I had reasons that make sense."

She stepped closer, and he had to adjust himself again. He couldn't help it when she was near, especially wearing a tiny outfit and covered in sweat. It did it for him.

She did it for him.

"I'm always confident. Though not when it comes to

you. Not lately. But that's something I need to work out on my own. I mean, if you don't like having sex with me and don't want to do it ever again, then fine. But maybe we can comment on it. Or…not. But what I came back here to tell you is that I'm sorry for hanging up. I was tired and whining, and I don't like when I act like that."

He had no idea where to start with that comment, but he spoke anyway. "You weren't whining. And I gave you cause to act however you wanted."

They were standing right in front of each other then, their bodies close but not touching.

"We keep calling each other best friends. And for so many years, we acted like it. We *were*. But for the past couple of days, we're not acting like it. And I know for a fact that being friends means standing by each other, even in the hard times. And, Loch? These count as hard times. Don't they? We should stick together when things aren't perfect."

Loch cursed under his breath, then cupped her face. He hadn't meant to touch her, then again, he hadn't meant to do a lot of things recently. "Ainsley."

Then he did the thing he shouldn't.

He kissed her.

Her tongue brushed along his, and he growled, deepening the kiss as he kept his hands on her face, needing to keep them there in case he moved too quickly, in case he scared either of them by doing what he shouldn't.

By stopping the denial.

When he pulled away, her eyes were wide, and they were both panting.

"Nothing's been perfect between us for a while, Ainsley, but that's not on you. It's me trying to keep my hands off you because you're one of the most important people in my life. And me and sex...we don't mix. My partners always leave, Ainsley. And I can't have you leave."

He hadn't meant to say those words, and knew he'd probably only confused her more, but it was the truth. He didn't have relationships with women. He wasn't a jerk, but he also didn't promise commitment. The only person he'd tried to do that with had left him. And left their daughter.

And Loch wasn't sure he could handle Ainsley leaving him. Wasn't sure he could handle her leaving Misty, even though he'd told her to stay away.

Because she would leave.

They all did.

"That doesn't make any sense, Loch." She licked her lips. "I'm not going anywhere."

Then she kissed him, pressing her body against his. She fit perfectly, a fit that made him think of other things.

Things far dirtier.

Then he remembered that she'd locked the door.

"I didn't plan this," she whispered against his lips. "I only wanted to talk."

He cupped her under her ass and turned them both around so she was sitting on the top of his desk, her legs spread, and his body between her thighs.

"This isn't going to solve anything, you know," she

whispered. She arched her neck, and he sucked on her delicate skin, needing her taste.

"It'll show you that I *liked* having sex with you. I had the best sex of my life with you. The fact that I stepped away? That's on me. It's only on me. It has to do with everything else going on around us. And the fact I don't want to lose you."

She bit his lip, and he growled. "You're not going to lose me. I can promise you that. Because I don't want to lose you either." He licked her lips, and she opened for him. "What are we doing, Loch?"

"I don't know, but I want to keep doing it."

She grinned. "It's the sports bra, isn't it?"

He bit her jaw. "It was the box jumps, wasn't it?"

"Maybe." A kiss. "This is stupid."

"Beyond stupid."

He kissed her again, and she tightened her legs around his body, pulling his dick close to the heat of her.

"But we're still doing it," she whispered. "Then, we'll talk."

He cupped her face and looked into her eyes, knowing he couldn't hide things from her. He'd always sucked at it, and he knew if he kept trying, he'd be the one watching her walk away.

"After."

Her eyes widened. "Promise?"

He could kick himself for the hurt he saw in her expression. "Yes. I promise." Then he took her mouth, needing her. They were at his damn workplace, and anyone could knock at any moment—and some would know *exactly* what they were doing in here. But he didn't care.

He had to have her, had to show her that he wanted her, that he cared for her, that he wasn't as much of an asshole as he had been lately.

So, he gave in.

And so did she.

He tugged on her sports bra, and she helped him take it off, not wanting to hurt her since the damn things always freaked him out. Then her breasts were right there, the pink-tipped nipples begging for his mouth. So he lowered his head and sucked on one, using his fingers to pluck at the other.

Ainsley gripped the edge of the desk, her legs around him as she let her head fall back. She looked like a fucking goddess, but she'd never believe him if he said that. She didn't take his compliments easily, and because he didn't speak unless it was important, he tended to hold back and not give enough.

That had to change.

With her in his arms, he knew that had to change.

"You're so fucking beautiful." Kiss. "I could taste you all day." Bite. "All fucking day." Suck.

"Loch. I need...I need..."

"I know what you need."

He stood up and cupped the back of her neck as he lowered his hands between her legs and over her yoga pants. Even through the fabric, he could feel the heat of her. He rubbed the heel of his hand against her, and she moaned, arching into him. So he did it again. And again.

And when she squirmed, he quickly moved back, tugged on the waistband of her pants, and grinned when she raised herself up off the desk, helping him take them off along with her panties in one go.

Then, his mouth was on her, licking and sucking at her cunt, alternating between breathing hot and blowing cool air over her when she rested her legs to his shoulders. He ate like a man at a feast, lapping her up as her arousal dripped down his chin, her pussy so wet and ready for him all he'd have to do is stand up and strip to slide right into her tight, hot, wet sheath.

But even though his cock was so hard he was afraid he'd pop in one go, he kept his mouth on her, looking up her sexy-as-sin body as she came on his face. Her body bucked so violently when he flicked his tongue over and over on her clit that he had to hold her down by the hips so she didn't fall off his desk.

Then he stood up, tore off his shirt, and shucked off his shorts before remembering he didn't have a very important thing they would need to continue this.

He cursed, gripping the base of his cock as he looked down at her coming off her high. He squeezed, trying to hold himself back from coming on her stomach right then and there just at the sight of her. He wasn't a teenager, he could last longer than this, but without a condom, they'd have to get a little more creative than they were already being.

She looked at him then, her pupils wide as she swallowed. "I'm clean. On the pill. I trust you, Loch. If you say you're clean, then you're clean. You're not going to let something happen to your body because you're stupid. You take care of yourself. Just like I do."

He leaned down and took her lips in a searing kiss. "I don't deserve you," he whispered.

"Same. Guess that makes us even. Now, please, get in me. Because you look like you're in pain standing there with that big cock of yours waiting for me." Then she spread her legs while still seated on his desk, and he was pretty sure he'd never seen anything so hot in his life.

He moved closer, placing the tip of his dick at her entrance. And when she met his gaze, he slowly slid inside, inch by inch, pulling out each time he pressed in a little more. Her breaths came in quick pants, and he groaned when she tightened her inner walls around him. As soon as he was fully seated inside her, he hooked her legs over his arms and *moved*.

He thrust in and out of her, hard and fast, no longer able to hold himself back. And, this time, he met her gaze without straying, without pulling away and flipping her over so it wouldn't be too much.

They'd already crossed that line. There was no going back.

She came first, her body shaking, her eyes rolling back, her breasts flushed, her nipples hard little points. And when she tightened even more around his dick, something he didn't think possible, he came as well, following her into the abyss.

Loch licked up Ainsley's neck again, their breaths mingling as they tried to come down from their high. He knew they needed to clean up, needed to talk, needed to do a lot of things, but when his cell vibrated on the desk, he knew their little bubble of just *them* was over. At least for now.

Ainsley's eyes danced with laughter as she met his gaze. "Answer it while you're still inside me. I dare you."

His softening cock twitched, and he met her gaze, a smile forming on his mouth. "You're bad."

She tightened her inner muscles, making his eyes cross.

"Fine." He picked up the phone, not bothering to look at the screen. "What?"

Ainsley slapped her hand over her mouth, holding back a giggle, and Loch couldn't help but want to thrust just a bit, but the voice on the other end made him freeze, the blood in his body icing over.

"Good to know you haven't changed, buddy."

"Riker," he growled. Ainsley gave him a weird look, and Loch knew he'd have to tell her about this man soon, but not when he was inside her, and not when he was dealing with this fucking dickhead.

"Ah, you remember me. You got my note?"

He'd known it.

"What the fuck do you want?" Loch slid out of Ainsley, not wanting her to be part of this any more than she already was. He met her gaze as he bent down to pick up his shirt so she could put it on. She did so, and he leaned down and brushed a silent kiss over her brow.

"I'm watching, Loch. And I think you know what I want."

Then, Riker hung up, and Loch almost threw his phone. Instead, he glanced at Ainsley and knew the time for secrets was over. The time for a lot of things was over.

Chapter 11

"*W*ho was that?" Ainsley asked, pulling the hem of Loch's shirt down. "And why do you look like you've either just talked to a ghost or you want to hit something. Maybe both."

Loch leaned down and kissed her quickly, surprising them both if the look in his eyes was anything to go by. She wasn't sure she'd ever get used to the idea that this was Loch or that they were doing this, but maybe she could.

Once they talked. Because that sounded like a conversation Ainsley really wanted to have. But they were going to talk no matter what. Now.

"Let's get cleaned up." He cleared this throat. "Then we'll go to my place so we can talk."

"And the phone call?" she pressed. "Is that going to be part of the conversation?"

"It's part of it." He closed his eyes and pinched the bridge of his nose. The fact that he was still naked in his office was not lost on her, and it was really hard to pay attention to the severity of the situation when his cock was still semi-hard, and she still had his semen inside her.

And on that note...

"Can I, uh...have a tissue or something?"

He cursed and then went to a cabinet, bringing out a clean towel. Then he slid between her legs, his eyes on hers as he gently cleaned her up. When he was done, he used the same towel to wipe himself down before tossing it into the trashcan next to his desk. Without another word, the two of them got dressed, her stripping off his shirt so he could wear it again. It felt weird to get back into sweaty clothes after everything that had just happened, but she had a feeling something even more important was yet to come that evening.

"Your house?" she asked.

"If that's okay. Do we need to stop by your place?"

She shook her head. "I have a change of clothes in my bag in the locker room, as well as some at your house. Though, when I locked the door, it was so we could talk, not so we could...you know." She knew she was blushing, but he wasn't smiling. Something was wrong, and she was finally going to find out what it was. "I hope the rest of the gym doesn't know what we were doing in here."

"My office is soundproofed." At her look, he shrugged. "We were trying out the tech for the security arm of the business. If anyone says anything, fuck them. Let's just get to the house. Okay?"

He was on edge, and not from what they'd just done. It had to be because of what they were going to talk about, as well as that phone call. So, when they quickly left his office and made their way to the locker rooms to grab their bags, she ignored any looks. Thankfully, she didn't think there were many, if any at all.

Loch talked to one of his guys at the front, and then they were at her car. "I walked," he said as he got into her driver's seat. She wasn't a fan of driving, so she didn't mind. It was Loch, after all, he liked being in control. And as she'd just had him inside her, proving that, it made sense.

She wasn't nervous, not really. Not when something was changing between them. So, when they got to Loch's place, and he told her to shower and change into her normal clothes while he did the same, she went about the motions, wondering what he could be hiding, grateful that he was finally going to tell her. They couldn't work it out if he kept it to himself.

The fact that something else could change between them after this had occurred to her as well, but she knew Loch. Loved him.

He meant something.

He meant everything.

And so does his daughter, she thought when she walked out and heard him talking to Misty on the phone. He was just hanging up when he caught sight of her and nodded.

"She was off to play with her grandma, and I didn't tell her you were here or I'd have let you talk to her. I want to get this over with."

She raised a brow. "Over with?"

"It's not an easy thing to go over, and it's complicated as hell, so I don't know where to start. But that means I just *need* to start. Okay?"

She reached forward and cupped his face. When he didn't pull back, she counted that as a win. "Okay. Tell me, Loch. Just…just tell me."

He blew out a breath. "Just don't hate me when I'm done." When she lowered her hand, they didn't move apart, remained so close that it was all she could do not to wrap herself around him and tell him that everything would be okay. She wasn't sure that was the truth anyway.

"I could never hate you." But she was still scared, that much she could admit to herself. If something had scared him enough to act this way, then she should be concerned, as well. "When I'm angry with you, and even the times I want to kick you in the shin for holding back and hiding… sometimes, I want to be able to hate you. but I can't." And maybe that was the problem.

Loch moved forward, tracing his finger over her cheek. She met his gaze, refusing to close her eyes and lean into him in case she missed something.

He studied her face for a few more moments before tugging her hand and bringing her to the couch. The same spot where he'd made love to her, *with* her. The same piece of furniture where they'd had endless nights of watching bad movies and bingeing TV shows. The same cushions where she'd splayed on top of him, wrung out after a particularly hard workout where he gave her no quarter. Where she cuddled with Misty, and where she watched Loch hold his baby girl after a long, sleepless night of cholic.

That couch held so many layered memories, but now she knew it might hold one more.

It was where he'd tell her what he'd been hiding.

Quite a lot of sentiment and meaning for a piece of wood and fabric.

"That phone call in the office, it was from someone I knew long ago. Someone I thought I'd left behind years ago." He frowned. "Turns out, I couldn't have been more wrong."

Ainsley reached out and gripped his hand, the calluses of his fingers under her palm reminding her that Loch had always worked with his hands. Had always been a man of his mind *and* his body.

"Just tell me."

"It's a long and complicated story, and I'm having trouble figuring out where to start."

"Then start chronologically. That's what I tell my students. Start at the beginning if you don't know how to set up an equation."

He gave her a small smile before his eyes filled with dread. Then he continued. "You know I used to work in security, but I was always vague on the details."

She knew her smile was weak, but it was real. "I always

thought you liked the idea that people thought you were a spy with a secret or something like that."

Loch shook his head. "No, not really. It was just…there wasn't much to tell. I used to be a hired bodyguard for those who needed me. I did recon and other missions that were legal, but most were for people with the type of money I could never hope to have. My boss and mentor, the owner of the company, taught me everything I knew and had strong morals. That meant we were never mercenaries or the type of guys you read about who take the wrong jobs and end up either getting innocent people killed or getting killed themselves."

He ran his thumb along her skin, and she swallowed hard, knowing this wasn't going to end well.

"Jason, my mentor, was a good man, but he didn't always hire good people. He brought in the best, and because he did that, sometimes, those people came with their own baggage. One of them, Riker, was a competitive asshole who was damn good at his job but didn't mind cutting corners. And he never said no to a job, no matter the danger or lines he'd cross to get it done."

At the mention of Riker's name, a chill slid down Ainsley's back, but she kept listening, knowing there was more to come.

"Riker was, *is* a mercenary. He wanted my job, wanted Jason's. He figured that if he kept in Jason's good graces, kept being the best, no matter the cost, he'd get the company once Jason retired and could use it for his own not-so-aboveboard purposes. I left because of Misty, but I also left because I didn't want to end up dead or in jail because Riker didn't know when to stop. Plus, that world is for younger men. I might not be old and have many years until I'll call myself that, but throwing my body headfirst into danger wasn't something I wanted to do. So, yeah, I came home and built the gym and the security business on the side to keep my family and friends safe from the dangers of the world…and the world I used to live in."

Ainsley frowned. "What do you mean by that?" She didn't like that he talked of his death as if it were almost a certainty. No wonder just the mere mention of Riker's name had made her want to burrow into Loch's side and never let go.

"I worked with some bad people. It didn't start out like that, but in the end, it's what happened. Jason let in the wrong people like Riker, and I've always been cautious about what I let out into the world. Hard to do when one brother was a cop whose injury and past cases got national attention, and when the other brother is a freaking reporter. Not to mention the fact that Tabby had issues out in Denver, and I could never go into hiding." He paused, looking into Ainsley's gaze. "Not that I would ever do that. My family is everything. That's why I left."

"But you're saying Riker and the others would want to…what? Hurt you? Because you left? But why?" She wasn't sure she was quite understanding, but then again, this wasn't her world, and she didn't know all the details.

"Me leaving could be part of it," Loch agreed. "Riker never liked losing. And he lost a lot when I was around. I was always Jason's number-two man and I had more clearance than he did. I didn't set out to be that way."

She shook her head. "You're Loch. Of course, you set out to be the best. You might not have thought you were doing it, but you don't like to lose, and you don't like to be second-best to even yourself. You put everything you have into whatever you're doing."

He snorted, giving her hand a squeeze. "That's true, though, in the end, I didn't want what Jason had. Yet Jason didn't agree, and Riker resented that. I'm no longer part of that life, even though I still have a few contacts. My life is now my family. My daughter. My work." He paused. "You."

She warmed from the inside but didn't say anything, knowing there was still more to come.

"Riker never understood that, but while he was always in the back of my mind, I moved on. I didn't want to be part of that life anymore, and I didn't let myself be. I figured Riker could have the company if he wanted. I told Jason my concerns, but my old mentor told me that everything would be okay. In the end, the only way to make that work for him was to, apparently, give me the fucking company."

Ainsley blinked. "What...what are you talking about?"

"Jason's dead," Loch said bluntly. "Didn't find out until I got a letter from a lawyer saying I now own the company and have some funds I didn't have before." He pinched the bridge of his nose again, and Ainsley moved closer so they were touching each other. His body radiated tension, and all she wanted to do was hold him and make everything better. But this was the real world, and that wasn't how things truly worked.

"I'm sorry," she whispered. She hadn't known about the man, Jason, before tonight, but Loch had called him a mentor. And from the pain in his voice, he was also a friend, and Loch grieved for the man. With everything else going on around them, however, she wasn't sure how much time he'd actually given himself to acknowledge that grief —if he had at all.

"I'm sorry, too." He lifted his arm, and she sank into him when he pulled her close, kissing the top of her head. "I'm sorry he's dead, and I'm sorry I don't know why. I called guys I know up there, and they thought it was natural causes. And as much as I want to believe that, there's some part of me that can't quite do that when Riker's in the picture."

She sighed. "Tell me."

"I don't know what happened to Jason, but I'll find out. I've talked to the authorities there, as well, but it'll take time. Until then? I have to figure out what to do with the company and the money I now have. I don't want any of it, Ainsley. Why didn't the man see that? Why didn't he see what I wanted when I left it all behind? Now, he's put it all on my shoulders when I never wanted any of it to begin with."

"What are you going to do?" She didn't know what

owning a company like that entailed, but she figured it was a lot of work and that nothing good could come of it. It didn't help that she had no idea what *the company*, as he called it, actually did. He was still being vague, but in a sense, she understood. Some things didn't need to have every detail laid out until it was absolutely necessary. The fact that he was talking about it now, even in *some* detail, meant that it was important.

"I'm going to dismantle and sell the damn thing. Close it. Whatever legally has to be done so it's not in my name and won't hurt anyone. Because while we might have done a lot of good, that kind of information—information that included the personal details and secrets of high-ranking people—in the wrong hands, in *Riker's* hands, could do a whole lot of bad. Someone could use Jason's good name to do some terrible things that I don't even want to think of. But, right now, I'm the owner, and I'm not dealing with it. Not yet. Because, first, I need to deal with what's going on in Whiskey."

She swallowed hard. "You're talking about Dennis." Somehow, she'd known all of it was connected.

He nodded. "The night I got the notice about the company, I also got a note I couldn't trace telling me that I needed to watch my back and that: *it will be mine*. As there's only one thing in my life right now that those words could allude to, I immediately thought of Riker. And as the investigation with Dennis continued, it started to point to that Riker was connected to that, as well. And then the call came in."

Ainsley sat up straighter. "You're saying Riker had something to do with Dennis's death? And that, what? He's *framing* you?"

"I don't know if Riker killed Dennis himself or if he's just using the other man's death to get at me. But, at first, I thought he had to have something to do with it. And after his phone call today? I *know* it."

"What did he want?"

"To tell me that he's watching me." He paused. "And that I know what he wants. I'm guessing the company... something I'm not going to give him."

"So that's why you pushed me away?" she asked. "Why Misty is with her grandparents? Because you're afraid of what Riker might do?"

He gave her a tight nod. "Misty is in a house I put the best security on. It's even better than mine because of the design of the house itself. She's safer there until I figure out what's going on. As for you. Hell, Ainsley, I thought if you weren't near me, you wouldn't be a target, but you're part of my life in every way. There's not much I can do to make it look like you aren't a part of me. And, yeah, there's a lot of other shit that we need to deal with between us, but I pushed you away because of Riker. I might be paranoid, but I want you safe."

"It's not being paranoid if they really *are* out to get you." She'd known there was a reason he'd hurt her, but he wasn't exactly forgiven yet. They had much more to talk about outside of what they had so far, but the fact that he'd trusted her with this much had to mean something.

Of course, it meant something.

She just had to protect her heart even as she fell just a little bit more for her best friend.

He kissed her then, making her toes curl.

"I don't know what's going to happen next. But I need you safe."

"If you need me safe, I need to not be in my head all the time, wondering what the fuck we're doing. So that might have to be something we actually talk about. Eventually." She hated even asking, but communication was key, and she wasn't about to be patted on the head and told that everything was okay.

"If I knew that, Ainsley, I wouldn't be as growly as I am."

She snorted. "You're always growly. So that's saying something. But, really, what are you going to do?"

"I'm going to kiss you."

Her skin heated. "Loch."

He let out a long breath. "I'm going to talk to the detectives again, tell them what might be happening, even though it's all far-fetched and doesn't make any sense. I didn't say anything before the call because it was all just conjecture. But, now? Well, it's still that, but now I have more in my mind saying it's connected. As for you? Hell, Ainsley, I couldn't walk away from you. I never could. I don't know what's going to happen next between us, but I can't stay away. So, if you'll have me, I'll try not to fuck things up more than I already have."

And when he kissed her again, she knew it was enough.

He was enough.

She just hoped she was, as well.

Chapter 12

*L*och held Ainsley close, his body fully awake even if his mind was just starting to wake up. It wasn't yet morning, not even close since he and Ainsley had just gone to bed, but she must have moved closer to him in the middle of the night, waking up a very important part of him.

A storm raged outside, lightning sparking across the sky with rain and snow pounding the windows. The fact that it was winter didn't mean anything, Thundersnow was a thing. Every once in a while, thunder boomed outside, and he would wake up, only to tug Ainsley tighter to his side. He hadn't realized how much he apparently needed her in his sleep, but then again, he'd told himself for so long that he didn't need her beyond what they had. Maybe he should have known this all along.

After he and Ainsley had talked, they'd gone to bed

without dinner, just lying there talking about everything else they hadn't said to each other before. They'd checked in with Misty and her grandparents again, though his daughter had already gone to bed before he called. Loch missed his daughter so damn much, and he had a feeling he'd be going to pick her up soon, no matter the deal he made with Marnie's parents. Ainsley was already deeply embedded into his life, and Riker, if he were truly watching as he'd said, would have already seen her. As for his daughter, she might be safer where she was, but damn it, he missed her.

Thunder rocked the house again. Ainsley moved even closer, and all thoughts of Riker and everything else fled Loch's mind. Instead, he slid his hand down and cupped the woman in his arms between her legs.

Ainsley moaned, and Loch gently bit down on her shoulder.

They were silent as he pulled her pants down, then his so they were skin-to-skin, his cock pressing against her ass. When she wiggled slightly, he grinned, moving his hands from her pussy to between them, his thumb sliding along her crease, dipping in to tease her ass. She froze, then looked over her shoulder.

"Loch?" she whispered.

"Next time." He wanted that ass of hers, and if she were willing, he'd get it.

She snorted. "Sure, honey."

He grinned, then bit down on her shoulder again before pulling back to rid her of the rest of her clothing.

He slowly raised her leg over his, his dick sliding along her wet heat. She was already soaking for him, ready. He had one hand around her front, cupping her breast, while the other was between her legs, playing with her clit as he slowly worked inside her, then out again, taking his time as they pleasured each other, getting to know one another in the dark—softly this time, rather than the heated and harder times of before.

When he pulled out of her fully, he moved her to her back, then slid inside again as she spread her legs. This way, he had more access to her mouth, her breasts, *her*.

They came together on a slow build, her breaths quickening as she came on him, and his seed filled her until they were both shaking, catching their breaths, and sweaty.

This was what Loch needed, what he wanted.

He'd wasted so much time being afraid to look at Ainsley this way, even a fraction.

He kissed her thoroughly, his softening cock still inside her as she pulled him against her, her breasts pressing against his chest when she wrapped her arms around him, her hands stroking lazily down his back.

He didn't want to waste any more time. He couldn't. Not when Ainsley was in his arms.

In his bed.

In his life.

Just…in him.

ANOTHER LIGHTNING STRIKE lit up the room and, this

time, the thunder followed straight after. The room shook, and then the hall nightlight Loch had for Misty went out, the rest of the house going dark immediately after, and the heat shutting off with a bang as a loud-as-hell sound came from the backyard, like something had exploded right next to his damn house.

"Damn it," Loch growled, pushing from the bed. Another streak of lightning hit the sky, and he looked down at Ainsley, the look in her wide eyes causing his chest to tighten.

"What was that?"

"I think the storm blew a transformer. I have a generator, but I need to go out and deal with it all. Jesus, I didn't realize the storm was going to be this bad." It was Pennsylvania, and where they were on the lower edge of the state, storms often passed over them even if the forecasters called for a blizzard. Sometimes, they stalled thanks to coastal winds and other crap and Loch ended up with a blown-out transformer and a dark house.

And possibly without security.

Fuck.

"I need to check the security system." He leaned down, kissed her hard on the mouth, and pulled on his jeans that he'd tossed on the chair next to the bed before he and Ainsley had gotten under the sheets. "Stay here with the door locked."

If possible, her eyes widened even more. "You don't think Riker has anything to do with this?"

Loch shook his head. "No, but I wouldn't put it past

him to use it to his advantage. Stay here. Stay safe. I'll be right back." He kissed her again, then headed out of his bedroom, closing the door behind him. Ainsley wouldn't do anything stupid. She might be bullheaded just like he was, but when it came to something important, she did the right thing.

The generator didn't start up, and that worried him since key parts of the house were connected to it, as well as his security system. He knew that Riker hadn't drummed up the storm as that was impossible and bordering on paranoia, but that didn't mean the other man hadn't done something to sabotage Loch's backup plans. Loch had been so distracted by dealing with everything the night before, he hadn't double-checked everything like he usually did. He'd made sure the alarm was set, but not his backup. Careless because he'd been wrung out, and Ainsley had needed to lie down, and he wanted to make sure she was safe and warm.

Fuck a dick. He hoped to hell and back that his distraction hadn't cost him anything because this was *not* the time to be lazy about the important things—including the safety of the woman he thought he might love more than just a friend.

Loch crept down his stairs, listening for anything out of the ordinary, but with the storm raging, he knew he'd be hard-pressed to hear anything out of place. It was probably something far less sinister than he was making it out to be, but it *was* the middle of the night, a storm was raging outside, seemingly trying to knock down the house, and a very warm and willing woman was up in his bed, probably scared out of her mind because Loch was overreacting.

Get a grip, he told himself. He didn't say it aloud in case his worries weren't, in fact, far-fetched. But, seriously, he just needed to get back upstairs to Ainsley, get a couple of more hours of sleep, then go and pick up Misty. The cops would be able to figure everything out with Dennis and whatever the hell had been going on around him, and he knew he was probably making things a far bigger deal than they needed to be. So what if Riker called and sent a note? That didn't make the man a murderer. It made him a pest that Loch would ignore as he got rid of his newly acquired company. Things weren't as dire as his bad feelings made them out to be.

Just as the thought crossed his mind, the sound of a window breaking in the living room hit his ears, and Loch whirled around, certain that it wasn't a branch that had done it. No, he *knew* he wasn't alone in the room, but it was too dark to see anything. Damn it. Arms out, body relaxed even though he was tense inside, he calmed his breathing and *listened*.

There.

He ducked as a fist came at him in the dark, punching out with his own to get the attacker in the gut. He ascertained that the person was a man thanks to the size of the barely perceptible shadow and the masculine groan when Loch made contact. Loch moved to the side as the intruder came at him again, this time catching Loch in the jaw. The guy was well trained, but from the size of the shadow and the skill of his moves, it wasn't Riker. It was someone else Loch knew from a distant past.

Chris.

Riker's second. Another asshole.

Chris bent low, going for Loch's knees, but Loch was faster. He shifted out of the way, knocking Chris down to the ground. Unfortunately for them both, the coffee table was in the way. Another loud crack filled the air as the wood top snapped in two, the weight of Chris's body too much for it to withstand since Loch had tossed him pretty hard.

Chris rolled to his feet and came at Loch again. This time, the moonlight barely peeking through the clouds and blinds glinted off something metal.

Fuck, the other man had a knife, and Loch wasn't armed since it was his own damn house and there wasn't supposed to be an intruder in the place.

Loch lunged out of the way as Chris moved forward, knife held out before him. From what Loch could remember, Chris was even more skilled with blades than he was, and time had seemed to only improve the other man's abilities. However, Loch would always be better at hand-to-hand than Chris. He'd need to remember that in order to get out of this alive.

Jesus. Had it been Chris all along with Riker just calling to make it sound like it was him? Or were the two working together? Loch didn't know, and he'd have time to think about it later. For now, he had to try and get out of this alive and make sure no one went up to find Ainsley.

Fuck, he hoped to hell Riker wasn't with Chris now, somehow going upstairs to where Ainsley was. Or even at Marnie's parents', trying to get at Misty.

A cold wash of fear and anger settled over Loch at that scenario, and then Loch wasn't thinking about what-ifs anymore. Instead, he became the man he used to be, the fighter he used to be, and he *moved*.

A hit to his side, a slice across his arm, a grunt, a scream, and then Chris was down on the floor, the knife skittering across the hardwood that led from Loch's living room to the kitchen. He hit Chris on the head, and the other man passed out. Loch searched the remnants of his broken coffee table for the zip ties he kept in a compartment that Misty never went into. He was always prepared just in case his past came back to haunt him.

And haunt him it did.

Sirens and lights blared in front of the house in the next instant, and Loch let out a breath, knowing that Ainsley had called the cops when she heard the sounds down below. Then he looked up and saw her at the top of the stairs in his shirt and her jeans, holding the baseball bat that he kept in his closet. Seven years of softball meant his best friend and lover knew how to use it. He was just a little pissed off that she'd come out of the bedroom at all. Not that he'd have been able to stay locked away during all of the noise and fighting either.

"Loch?" Ainsley's voice shook, but she still sounded strong. Ready.

Was it any wonder he loved her?

He'd think about that thought later. First, he needed to make sure his woman and his daughter were safe.

"Ainsley. You safe?

She came downstairs fully then, the spotlights and flashing lights from the front yard casting shadows over her face. Her eyes narrowed on his arm. "You're bleeding, so I guess I need to be the one asking that question."

He looked down at the cut on his arm and shook his head. "It's shallow, doesn't even need stitches. Stay where you are. There's glass and pieces of wood all over the floor, and I don't want you to hurt yourself. You the one who called the cops?"

She nodded. "I heard the shouts and called right away. Was I supposed to?"

"I'm not in a secret organization or Batman, Ainsley. Always call the cops for intruders. I didn't right away because my security system is down and I was a little busy knocking Chris on his ass."

"You know his name? It's not Riker?"

"I'll tell you everything later." A knock sounded on the door, and he sighed. "And I'll be telling them everything, as well."

There was no use hiding anything anymore, especially since the connections he'd thought he put together had been flimsy before but were anything but now.

BY THE TIME the cops left, Chris in tow, Loch had a headache from hell and a bandage on his arm. Like he'd thought, he hadn't needed stitches, even though the blood had worried Ainsley. Now, he and Ainsley were sitting on his couch, the place once again clean since they hadn't wanted to keep any of the debris around after the cops did what they needed to do with the evidence. The power had come back on about an hour ago, and Loch had been able to set up his security system and backup again. Chris had cut a wire to the backup, but that had been easily fixed.

Now, Fox and Dare were in his house, having rushed over when Ainsley called them out of their beds. Loch had been in the middle of getting grilled by Renkle when they arrived, even though this clearly hadn't been his fault. The detectives seemed to understand that now. Ainsley had known exactly who Loch needed at the house and what to do. She'd also called Marnie's parents, waking them up to check in on Misty and their house. Somehow, she'd managed to calm them down and not rile them up, making everything sound as if she were just worried about the storm and not something worse. Ainsley hadn't had much contact with the older couple in the past since things were always slightly strained when it came to his friendship with Ainsley, but that hadn't seemed to matter when she called to make sure his little girl was okay.

Somehow, he would have to explain to Misty and Marnie's parents about his new relationship with Ainsley, as well as some of the dangers going on around them. But that time would come, and it would not be at five in the morning after a horrible storm and a break-in at his home.

"This is ridiculous," Dare muttered from his side,

drinking coffee to keep himself awake. All of them were chugging the stuff, though he had a feeling he and Ainsley didn't need the caffeine, their adrenaline running hot enough for seven cups of coffee. "What does your old buddy have to gain by either using Dennis's death to his advantage or doing it on his own? You're not going to give him the company's contacts because he's threatening you. If anything, you'd hold them back even more because you don't take threats."

Loch shrugged. "I didn't say the other man was sane or that any of this made any sense. But he comes at my family? My kid?" His gaze flittered over to Ainsley before going back to Dare. "Anyone I care about? It might make me pause. And he knows that."

"You're not going to let him get away with this. The cops aren't either." Ainsley folded her arms over her chest, still wearing his shirt. His brothers had noticed, but he didn't care. They knew that he and Ainsley had changed their relationship, so it shouldn't have been a surprise.

"I know. I don't know what's going to happen next, but we'll take care of it." Loch let out a breath. "I'll keep you safe. And because I know you're worried, Fox, I'm not going to cross any legal or ethical lines. The cops can handle the investigation. I'm going to work on keeping my family safe." And his family included Ainsley, and he knew she knew that. He'd just do his best to make sure she understood the ramifications of it. Because she was his now, and that meant he wasn't going to let go. She'd said she wouldn't leave him like the others did, and he'd just have to trust her on that.

Because she was his.

And that meant he had to keep her safe.

And in his life.

No matter what.

Chapter 13

*A*insley rubbed her temples, the fact that she hadn't gotten enough sleep the night before starting to wear on her as the day progressed. When she was in Loch's arms after talking late into the night as the storm started up, she'd slept hard as if she'd known she would be safe no matter what happened outside of his hold. And, as it turned out, that had been the case. Her safety and life were never in jeopardy with Loch near. He was able to take care of anything in his path. The fact that he'd had to do that at all, though, didn't make her feel like roses. And fear still slid through her when she thought about what could have happened if Loch hadn't been able to subdue the intruder like he did.

How was this her life? How on earth did all of this happen in such a short time? She was just getting used to the fact that she and Loch had *finally* taken a step toward something new and real when all of its twists and turns kept interrupting.

That was what real life was, though, she guessed. Twists and turns and trying to catch up while living in the moment.

Loch and his brothers had talked things over as the sun came up. Now, no amount of coffee was going to help the fact that she'd only gotten a couple of hours of sleep before she and Loch had woken up in each other's arms, had the sweetest and hottest sex of her life, and then had been pulled out of bed by hell.

Apparently, Chris—and maybe even Riker from what Loch had said—had sabotaged the generator and used the storm as a convenient way to break in. Loch had figured that Chris or Riker would have broken in on their own later if the power hadn't gone out thanks to the thunder-snow. That meant that someone had been watching the house. And when she'd mentioned that she thought she'd seen someone outside the window when she was at Melody's, Loch had blown a gasket. She didn't know what he was planning, but she had a feeling that other than for work after this, she wouldn't be left alone for long. As it was, Loch was at the police station, giving another state-ment and relaying all the information he could while she was at home, locked up and secured behind the security system Loch had put in the year before. She had papers to grade, but she knew she wouldn't be able to focus on them as much as she should.

With all the issues going on with Loch and her, she'd forgotten the date.

She never forgot the date.

And, because of that, the guilt of doing so, of not being enough when she was younger, piled together, and she suddenly didn't want to talk to anyone. She wanted to wrap herself in blankets and forget that the world was horrible for just a moment.

But it wasn't as if she could do that.

As if on cue, her phone rang, and she knew without even looking at the readout who it would be. Her mother only called on certain days, and today would be one she wouldn't forget—even if it had slipped Ainsley's mind for a few hours.

The guilt hit her again, and she answered the phone, trying to keep her voice calm and collected.

"Hi, Mom."

"Ainsley." A strained pause. "How are you?"

Her mom didn't live in Whiskey and wouldn't have heard about any of the recent goings-on. For that, Ainsley was grateful. She loved her mom, she really did. The other woman was her only family left, and Ainsley would never forget that, but she also knew that every time her mother finished a conversation with Ainsley, she'd go into herself and hide, letting the depression take over. It wasn't her fault, it wasn't anyone's fault.

It was just that they weren't the family they once were, and the pain and loss shared between them was sometimes too much for anyone to bear.

"I'm…I'm okay." Not quite a lie, but not quite the truth either. And it wasn't even because of everything that had happened the night and week before.

Ainsley had forgotten the day.

How could she have done that?

"I'm okay, too," her mother when on. "I'm just calling, well…you know why I'm calling." A pause as Ainsley knew her mother was likely holding back tears. They were doing better, far better over the years, but today and the other day that was important for this moment would always be difficult for the two of them. "I visited her this morning when I woke up. Are you going later? I can join you if you want."

Ainsley was already shaking her head even before she said she would be fine. Visiting her sister's gravesite was hard for Mom, and it wasn't something they did often. For a couple of years after Katie had died, Ainsley and her mother had regularly gone to visit her to leave flowers and just to talk. But flowers were for the living, the same with headstones and manicured plots. Recently, when they were talking over beers, Ainsley had told Loch that, when she died, she wanted to be cremated after her organs were put to good use.

"I want to fly on the wind," she'd said to him, her tone a whisper. "I don't want to take up space."

Loch had reached out and gripped her hand, giving it a squeeze. "You never take up space, Ainsley."

"Then, when I die, will you take me to a place you love and set me free?"

He'd given her a strange look. "If that's what you want, but why do you think I'd outlast you?"

She hadn't known what he'd meant by that. Perhaps that he'd go before her, or maybe now it was because it would be too hard. She understood. Saying goodbye was never easy, but saying goodbye far too soon broke something deep inside.

"I'll go later today. We got a bit of snow," she added, then held back a sigh since her mother had come to Whiskey for the grave. She'd have seen the snow.

"I saw. The roads weren't too bad, though. The city takes care of everything nicely. Her birthday is always the hardest, but I tell you that every year, don't I? All the anniversaries, the first times, the tenths, it all adds up, but the birthdays are the hardest."

"I know." And she did. Katie's birthday meant that she wasn't around to see it, wasn't around to reach that age.

Katie had been ten when she died of a heart condition no one knew she had. She'd been healthy and active, if a little more of a bookworm than even Ainsley. Ainsley was six years older, just out of the age range where they were best friends, but she'd adored her little sister. And because Mom had become a single mother when Dad ran out on them, she'd had to work the night shift as well as a few day shifts, as well. That left Ainsley to watch over Katie, to make sure she ate and did her homework. She was there for bedtimes and bad dreams. She had been there for many of Katie's firsts, had captured many of them on tape for their mom.

Ainsley had been alone in the house when Katie went to sleep with a chest cold and never woke up.

She'd been alone in the house when she had to call 911 and beg for them to help her sister. Tabby and her family, Loch included, had shown up even before Ainsley's mom because they had been closer and hadn't been working.

Mom had never forgiven herself for not being there that day.

But Ainsley had never *once* blamed her mother for it. Mom worked overtime every week to make sure there was food in their bellies and a roof over their heads when Dad left them with nothing, stripping their bank accounts and school funds on his way out the door. And every time Mom was home, even if she was exhausted with dark circles under her eyes, she put her daughters first. She had given everything for her little girls.

But Katie had died anyway.

And Mom and Ainsley hadn't been able to mend what they had, their bond ripped to shreds by the loss. Not because of blame, never that, but because the memories were too crisp. Too painful.

Ainsley had finished school, gone to college, and had grown up, getting close to Loch and his family along the way. And Mom had closed in on herself, trying to reach out but never really able to. Ainsley didn't know what their relationship would have been like if they were able to stay close when their world was pulled apart, but she knew that staying together, staying close, *hurt*. Not just her mom, but Ainsley, too.

Because every time she heard her mom's voice, she remembered the keening wail as they told her that Katie was dead.

Ainsley heard the tears and sobs of when she was younger when Mom had tried to hide them from her and Katie while she was in the shower.

Mom had tried to shield them from everything. But, in the end, it hadn't been enough.

So, no, Ainsley didn't blame her mother, but she also didn't know her all that well these days.

Her mom cleared her throat, and Ainsley realized they'd been silent for an awkwardly long time while she'd been in her head.

"So, anything new going on with you? Are you seeing anyone?"

Her mom was trying to change the subject, and while Ainsley understood, it was always awkward. As much as Ainsley wanted to fix the rift between her mom and her, she wasn't sure they could or even should. Some pain was too much to bear, and while she loved her mother, she didn't know what to do when it came to her anymore.

Ainsley had latched on to the Collins family, and maybe that made her a bad person, perhaps she was running away, but her mother was healthier and happier when they weren't best friends.

And for that reason alone, Ainsley would do everything she could to make sure things stayed the way they were.

"I'm seeing someone new," she said carefully. "Um, I'm seeing Loch, actually." She wouldn't mention everything else going on or the danger that had come at them since she didn't want to worry her mother, but Mom knew Loch. Mom loved Loch even if she didn't see him often since she didn't see *Ainsley* often. It was better that way. Safer. Healthier.

"Really?" For once, her mom's voice brightened. Even on this day of all days, her mom sounded *happy*. "Oh, Ainsley. I love him for you. You're such good friends, and there's something between you…well…I'm happy for you, baby." A pause. This one longer. "Katie would have been happy for you, too. Remember when she met him the first time and she just stared at him, her eyes wide with so much puppy love? She was so adorable, and he was so good with her."

Ainsley had forgotten that day since it had been so long ago, but now she smiled, her heart warming. "I remember. I'm going to have to ask Loch if he remembers. Because I also had a crush on him, though I was too young for him at the time."

"I hear a smile in your voice, baby. That's good. He's good."

The two of them talked for a few minutes longer, the conversation going much better than any of their previous talks. And though it hurt to remember the day, the phone call gave Ainsley hope.

Once she'd hung up, Ainsley packed up her things and bundled up. She needed to visit Katie's grave and she needed to do it alone. It was the middle of the day. No one would come after her, not when they seemed to want Loch and not her, no matter how protective the man was.

She wasn't going to let the world take away the one day she needed to be with her sister, even if it was a symbol for the living and not truly Katie.

So, Ainsley left Loch a message since he hadn't answered his phone and headed to the graveyard herself. Her mom had been right in saying that the roads had been cleared. They hadn't been tended too well in the neighborhoods when Loch made sure she got home, but in the hours since, the sun had risen, and a lot of the snow had already melted.

Though Ainsley knew that others were around since this was a rather large cemetery, right then, with the snow piled up around her, the soft mounds untouched by people or even animals all unmarked and pristine, it felt like she was all alone in the world. And that's exactly what she needed right then.

Solitude.

She made her way to Katie's grave, following the only other footsteps along the cleared path. Her mother's if she were guessing correctly. Surely others would have walked through the site, but none had ventured this way yet other than her mother on her way to visit Katie for her birthday. Ainsley would do the same. She would talk and maybe cry. She'd try to laugh, but she'd have to remember that Katie wasn't there anymore. Speaking to her as if she were around was more for Ainsley's benefit than Katie's, but the idea of being forever lost to others always made Ainsley cold inside, so she liked to think that Katie was listening from wherever she was.

And probably laughing at the ridiculousness that was Ainsley's life.

They hadn't had much money when Katie died, and to be honest, Ainsley and her mother didn't have a lot of money *now*, but they'd had enough to get a small stone for their Katie.

Katie Michelle Harris
Our baby girl.

Ainsley went to her knees, ignoring the cold and wet on her pants, and wiped the snow off the stone. Her mother had gotten most of it before, but since Katie was under a tree, a place she'd loved when she was alive, some of the snow from the branches had fallen.

"Miss you," Ainsley said softly. "I always do. And, like always, I never know if I should tell you happy birthday or not. You should be here, though. I always sound like a child when I say it isn't fair, but it isn't. You should be here with me, annoying Mom and being the adorable self you were. I don't say *are* anymore, I'm getting better at my tenses after all this time. I know I talk to you when I'm at home, or while I'm teaching. Or when I'm trying that dance class I know you're laughing at me over. I talk to you when I'm with Loch and when I'm just thinking about him —which seems to be often. But talking to you here hurts more, though I know it shouldn't. I know you're not in pain, but I guess I'm the one left behind, the one in pain. And I hate it. I hate this for you, but maybe there's something else beyond this that is so much greater than this pain, and you're the one waiting for me. I'd like to think that."

Ainsley talked about her students, her home, Loch's family, Misty, all of it. She told Katie about silly things that had happened in the months since she'd last come to the stone.

"I'm with Loch," Ainsley whispered. "You probably already know that, but it happened. I've loved him forever, Katie. Or at least what seems like forever. And it seems so weird that it took this long, while at the same time I don't believe it's real. I want it to be real. I want it to be forever because I've always wanted a forever. I know you didn't get one, and I'll always hate the part of life that took you away from us, but just know I love you, okay? And I love him, too, but in a way where I hope that he doesn't break a part of me." Ainsley let out a sigh. "That's probably a little too much information, but you're here and, well, if you were *really* here, I'd probably be telling you this anyway. I love him, Katie. With everything that I am. I don't know what's going to happen next, but I hope there's a future for us. I love that little girl of his, and I love the idea we could be a family. I know it's all too new, but I've had him in my life for what seems like forever. And I want more of it."

Ainsley let out a sigh.

"But, first, we need to take care of what's coming at him—at us."

Ainsley told her sister about everything that had been

happening with Dennis and the others. What had happened the night before at Loch's house. Everything.

She missed her sister but knew that dwelling on the past and the what-ifs wasn't healthy, another reason she didn't come to the gravesite often. Today, however, was exactly what she needed. She needed to breathe, to remember that the world was more than the tension that had been going on around her recently.

Then, as soon as she thought that, a branch cracked behind her, and she whirled to look, only to let out a gasp as something slammed into the side of her head, knocking her to the ground. Her vision went hazy for a moment, and then she couldn't see anything.

There was only darkness.

Chapter 14

"*A*insley, baby, wake up." Loch's voice shook as he spoke, his hands cupping Ainsley's face as he tried to wake her up.

He'd come to the graveyard after hearing her message once he left the station, knowing exactly where she'd be on this day at this time. He should have thought of it before he left her alone so he could have come with her, but he'd had other things on his mind.

Now, he just hoped to hell his lack of foresight hadn't cost her everything.

"Loch?" Her eyelashes fluttered as she opened her eyes, even as she spoke. "Did someone hit me?"

He cursed under his breath, thankful that there wasn't any blood beneath her on the snow. He'd never forgive himself if she bled because of him. He wasn't going to forgive himself as it was.

"Looks like it. I called the cops already, and since I was just *there*, they're on their way. Jesus, Ainsley. Are you okay? What happened?"

She waved him off, trying to sit up. "Let me sit up," she begged when he held her down on his lap.

"I need to hold you for a bit, and in case you have a concussion. Let's just keep you steady."

"I'm fine. Just a little sore from whoever came up from behind and hit me." She paused, her eyes going unfocused for a moment. He hoped she was just remembering something and not truly hurt, because he wasn't sure his heart could take that. "I was all alone for the whole time. The only footprints in the snow were my mom's since she called and said she had already come by."

He nodded, frowning since he knew Ainsley was never okay on this date, and really not okay after talking to her mom. Add to that the fact that she was just attacked, and it was all he could do not to bundle her up and take her home, keeping her locked away from anyone who could hurt her.

"There was a sound like someone stepping on a twig, and as I turned, I saw a blur of movement, and then my head hurt." She touched her head and paused. "And then…you were here. How did you find me?"

"You called and left a message. Plus, if I would have looked at the date earlier, I would have known where you were."

I know you.

He didn't say it, but he thought it, and from the look in her eyes, she understood.

He cupped her face, lowering his head to brush his lips against hers. He'd picked her up slightly so she was lying on him and not the melting snow, but he wanted to get her someplace warm soon. Thankfully, he could hear a siren in the distance so he knew the authorities would be there soon —hopefully with the ambulance he'd requested. Considering they had seen him yesterday at his house and just a bit ago at the station, he was getting a little too familiar with the local authorities.

"I'm so damn sorry," he whispered, his head bent low as the others came closer.

"It wasn't your fault."

He didn't agree, but he didn't have time to say anything else. By the time they were questioned, *again*, and Ainsley was set to rights with only a bump on the head and thankfully not a concussion, Loch was past being on edge and wanting to be home and out of the bitter wind.

The two detectives who seemed to be everywhere Loch was these days didn't act as if they thought it was Loch, and for that, he was grateful. After Loch had given them all the information he had about his past and possible motives, and after the incident at his house, he had a feeling they were finally on the same page.

He just didn't know if it was going to help since Riker always seemed three steps ahead of him.

It had to be Riker. Chris wasn't saying anything, at least

from what Loch had gleaned from the police, but Loch knew that Riker was behind it all.

And the man was watching.

Because either Riker had another partner, one who wanted the company in Riker's hands for God only knew what reason, or Riker had attacked Ainsley himself. There was no way it wasn't connected. It was all a message.

And that meant Loch needed to keep his family safe. Close. And protected.

They were on the way to his place, having left Ainsley's car in the lot. Fox and Dare had said they'd take care of it for him soon, and it was all Loch could do to not break the damn steering wheel off in his rage.

"You're moving in with me," he said out of the blue through gritted teeth.

"What?" Ainsley asked, her voice a little high-pitched. "That...what?"

He held back a curse. He needed to coax her into it, make her see that it was for her safety and not because he was once again dramatically shifting their relationship—though that would be a byproduct. He didn't know when everything had gotten so complicated, but then again, when it came to him and Ainsley, it was always complicated.

He let out a breath, trying to calm his heart as he turned into his drive. "You're staying here with me. For your safety." He paused. "With Misty too since I'm getting her from her grandparents' today." He turned off the car and looked at Ainsley. "Riker and his men know you belong to me."

"Oh, really?" She arched a brow and didn't for one instant look like a woman who'd just been hit on the head in a damn graveyard. Instead, she looked like his Ainsley, sarcastic and fucking beautiful.

He closed his eyes for a moment, praying for patience. He didn't have much, especially when it came to the idea that Riker could hurt those he loved. "You know what I mean."

"I don't, but let's move on. That's what we do best." She gave him a look, and he winced. Yeah, they needed to talk some more about what they were doing together, but first, they had to stop whatever the hell Riker was doing.

"You'll be safe at my house."

"Yeah, because being at your house was so safe for you last night." Anger flashed in her eyes, and he knew she was thinking about the bandage on his arm under his coat. It didn't hurt, but she'd told him that she didn't like seeing him bleed. And, hell, his heart had almost stopped when he saw her prone on the ground in front of Katie's grave. They were even then, though he wasn't going to say that. The fact that it was even an idea made him want to find Riker and strangle him. Going by the book and the law wasn't making things easier, but he wasn't going to become a vigilante, he was just going to keep his family safe.

"The house is good. I fixed everything and will be adding an additional layer of security today after I pick up

Misty. It won't happen again." That was a vow he'd do anything to keep.

"So says every murder podcast I've listened to. I want to stay sexy. I don't want to get murdered."

"If you bring up that murderino shit one more time…"

She gave him a smile that said they weren't finished, but joking about silly things was the only way to break the tension. "Whatever. I'll stay with you because I believe you and, yeah, your house is theoretically safer than mine. But something needs to happen because I'm scared, Loch. I don't like being scared."

He leaned over and kissed her then, cupping her face as gently as he could. "Let me take care of you."

"You always do, Loch. Just remember, I need to take care of you, too."

The two of them made their way inside the house, Loch triple-checking security before he called Marnie's parents. Instead of him driving to them, they were going to drop Misty off, wanting to see him, as well. They didn't know everything going on, but they were worried and were damn good people—even if their daughter wasn't.

It was weird that he didn't even consider contacting Marnie to tell her that her daughter was safe. There was no need, and he had no idea where she was anyway. Her parents might have a number for her, but it was constantly disconnected, her address ever-changing. Marnie literally had nothing to do with Misty's life, and Loch was fine with that. Misty had women in her life she could look up to, and two sets of grandparents she loved.

And she had Ainsley.

A fact that he had almost ruined because he'd been too fucking scared to face reality and take a chance.

Standing in his bedroom, he pulled Ainsley closer, holding her to his chest.

"What's wrong?" she asked. "Besides the obvious."

"I'm sorry for pushing you away. It was a gut reaction because things were changing…and because of Riker. I can't believe I did that. Even if you and I weren't…doing what we are, I never should have threatened to pull you out of Misty's life. It might get even more interesting when she finds out we're dating, but that's something we'll work on together. There's no way I can separate you two. And the fact I thought I should in order to protect her, to protect *me*, just goes to show you that I'm a fucking idiot some-times. Well, most of the time if you listen to my brothers and Tabby."

"I wasn't going to let you take that little girl from my life, Loch. It might have changed things if I was out of *your* life, and I would have broken a bit inside by losing you, but there was no way I wouldn't have fought for her. For you."

He kissed her then, needing her so much he could barely breathe. "Never again. I don't know what's going to happen with us, but know this, no matter what, Misty will always be in your life. You make her smile, make her laugh. You give her something I can't. And I don't want to break that."

She searched his eyes with her own, and he kissed her again. "You say no matter what happens. But, Loch? I don't want to lose you either. You're my best friend. Remember that."

"I do. Always."

Then his mouth was on hers, and her hands were under his shirt, skin-to-skin, breath-to-breath.

"Are you too hurt to do this?" he asked. "We have an hour until Misty gets here."

Her eyes sparkled. "Just be gentle."

"For you, I can try."

She reached up and bit his jaw, and he knew it might take effort for him to try, but for Ainsley, he'd tie himself down before he hurt her. He slowly stripped her of her clothes, taking care not to touch the bump on her head, and then he stood back, and she stripped him of his, her hands shaking as she reached his belt buckle, but he knew it wasn't from pain or even nervousness.

The anticipation sparking between them was what moved them forward.

It was the antidote to his pain: his need.

She was his everything.

She wrapped her hand around his cock, giving him a squeeze before pumping a few times. His eyes crossed, and he groaned but didn't step away, loving her hands on him. When she started to go to her knees, however, he stopped her.

"I don't want you to hurt your knees."

"But I want to taste you."

He licked his lips then picked her up, carrying her to his bed. "Then let's do it this way because the idea of your mouth on my dick is something I've thought about for far too long." He settled her on the edge of the bed as he moved to get comfortable in the middle. "But if you're going to taste me, I want to taste you at the same time. So, it's up to you if you want to ride my face, or we go side by side."

She blushed even as she licked her lips. "You say the sweetest and sexiest things."

He wasn't normally like this, had never been *that guy*. But for Ainsley? Yeah, he'd be that guy. "Just for you."

"You better. And I don't know if I can straddle you and reach your dick since you're so much bigger than me." She gave his dick a pointed look. "Well, you're big all over. Aren't you?"

"Now you're the one saying the sweet and sexy things."

They moved so they were on their sides and, soon, his mouth was between her legs, and she was giving his cock tentative licks before she sucked him into her mouth. He groaned, almost losing his concentration when it came to eating her up, drip by drip, lick by lick when she hollowed her mouth and flattened her tongue on his tip.

When she sucked on his balls then cupped them in her hand as she swallowed as much of him as she could, he almost came right then but forced himself to hold back since she hadn't come yet. He licked her clit, gently biting down as he used her wetness to play with her back hole. She sucked in a breath, pressing into his hand as he used his forefinger to gently breach her entrance.

"Loch," she gasped, pulling away from his dick.

"Too much?"

She shook her head, licking down his shaft. "Not enough."

He grinned, then worked more of his finger inside her, pulling out as he used his other hand to play with her pussy, lowering his head to lick her at the same time. He worked her, loving her taste, the way she gasped when he moved just right. And when she came, he lapped her up, wanting every drop of her and not intending to miss anything.

He almost came again when she tightened her grip on him, but he pulled away and maneuvered them both so she was straddling him, her breasts bouncing from the movement. And since they were there, and he could never get enough of her tits, he cupped them in his hands, pressing them together and brushing his thumbs over her tight nipples.

"I wasn't done," she said with a gasp when he filled her with his cock in one thrust. "Jesus. You're so fucking big. I forget sometimes."

He grinned, slowly sliding in and out of her as she rocked back and forth over his dick. "And you're wet and tight. Not going to last long."

"As I was trying to get you to come in my mouth, you better be close."

"Come here and kiss me, taste yourself on my tongue." And she did, still moving her hips with his as they fucked, slowly and softly, yet just a little hard like they liked it.

She came again, and he followed her, his climax so

intense he knew he'd release everything inside of him just by her touch alone.

This woman was his.

His to love.

His to protect.

His to cherish.

His.

And he'd do anything in his power to keep her that way.

Anything.

Chapter 15

*a*insley was sore, and not just from getting hit on the head earlier that day. No, Loch had done his best to make sure she was loved in every possible way before Misty's grandparents dropped her off, worry and love in their gazes.

Misty had taken one look at Ainsley and had run to her, full-tilt with her arms outstretched. Ainsley had hugged her tightly, her love for the little girl unending. She hadn't missed the glances between Misty's grandparents, but they hadn't been looks of anger. Instead, Ainsley thought it could have been more shared grief, the fact that their daughter wasn't there to be a part of this. It was Marnie's loss, but Ainsley wasn't going anywhere, and neither were Misty's grandparents. They'd find a way to make it work because even with that glance, they hadn't acted as if they didn't want Ainsley around. They never had. They'd been gracious and loving, even if they weren't as emotive as Loch's parents.

Misty was one very lucky girl, even without Marnie in her life. And though Ainsley would never speak it aloud, she thought that Misty was probably even luckier that Marnie *wasn't* around.

That might make Ainsley a bad person, but the fact that Misty had never known her mother meant the little girl couldn't miss her as much as she might if Marnie had left later in Misty's life. Ainsley knew things were going to get harder as Misty grew up, but Loch's family, Misty's maternal grandparents, and Ainsley herself would find a way to heal those wounds. No matter what.

Now, however, was the time for them to pretend that everything was fine for Misty's sake as they sat in Loch's parents' home and had a Collins family dinner. Ainsley had been invited for years and came often, but this was the first time she was coming *with* Loch rather than just as his best friend.

To say that she was nervous was an understatement.

Add in the fact that she knew the adults would want to talk about what had happened throughout the week, and she knew it would be a long dinner, if a delicious one.

Since the night had been planned before she and Loch had slept together, before the murder, the attack, well… before everything that seemed to change on a dime, Ainsley had to get to the house early since she and Fox were cooking. That meant that Loch and Misty got there early too since they were riding together.

Like a family.

Nope, not thinking about that. Too much, far too soon. They might be living together for the moment, might be acting like they were further into their relationship than they were, but it was because of the circumstances. The fact that they already had the base of their relationship helped, but everything else going on around them was what had made it all feel so much more urgent, so much more...developed.

So, no, Ainsley wouldn't be thinking about that.

Instead, she and Fox would be using what they'd learned during their cooking classes and would make dinner for everyone at the elder Collinses' home. Ainsley would never forget when Loch had found out that she and Fox were taking the classes. She and Fox had wanted to keep it a secret since, first, it was kind of embarrassing that they needed so much extra help to just cook basics, and secondly, it was something just for her. And Fox, of course, but mainly something just for her. She and Fox had been walking out of class one night, and Melody and Loch had seen them. Melody hadn't thought anything of it. Had thought she and Fox were just friends, even though Ainsley knew Fox had explained it.

Loch had gotten oddly jealous, and Ainsley had just brushed it off at the time.

But now...maybe she shouldn't have.

It didn't matter, though, because Fox and Melody were engaged and having a baby and Ainsley and Loch were...

well, they *were*. She hated titles, but she guessed he was her…boyfriend? See, titles sucked.

And tonight was about family. About dinner. And about trying to calm down after a hectic and dangerous week.

"You look nervous," Fox said from her side. "Is it because you're a better cook than I am and you're afraid I'll hurt you while we do this? Or is it because this is a meet-the-parents night where the parents already know you?"

Ainsley looked over her shoulder and glared at Fox. "It's no wonder you're the younger brother. Pest."

He just grinned. "Tabby's younger than me. You, too. But, yeah, your Loch-y boy is the big, grumpy brother. And even with all the shit going on with him, he's still smiling. I'm going to go out on a limb and thank you for that."

She leaned against the kitchen counter, aware that she couldn't rest for long since Barbara Collins would be in the kitchen at any moment to check on them. The fact that Loch's mother had given up her space at all for Ainsley and Fox to try out their cooking skills for dinner either meant she'd lost a bet or actually believed something amazing could come out of this kitchen.

Or…there were emergency lasagnas in the freezer.

Either way, Ainsley was just happy that she could try to do something for the family who had taken her in when she'd thought she'd lost everything—including a mother who hadn't been able to remain whole for her remaining daughter.

"You're a menace, but I'm glad Melody loves you."

Fox's grin was wide then, his eyes bright. "She's pretty amazing, isn't she? And did you see her today? Her bump is bigger, though when I told her that, she kicked me in the shin."

"Fox."

"I know. I know. You never tell a woman she's bigger than she was the day before. But it's our baby. There should be a rule or something that it's okay to say that when it's your baby."

"Fox."

"Fine."

Ainsley just grinned. Arguing with Fox was fun because he usually did all the talking. She just had to give him a look, and he understood what she meant.

"Now, we're making mashed potatoes, roasted chicken, two veggies, rolls, and the pie you and Melody made yesterday, which is already sitting on the counter. We can do this." She paused, suddenly unsure. "Right?"

"The chicken is already in the oven, stuffed with oranges, a lemon, and butter. We did that, and we didn't break anything. We're good. Now, on to the sides. The rolls are rising, and I didn't end up with flour all over my face, so I'm counting that as a win."

She didn't mention that he had some in his hair, but she was pretty sure she had some in hers, as well.

"Let's get back to it then."

They laughed as they got back to work, Barbara coming in to check on them a few minutes later. She sweetly brushed the flour out of Fox's hair, then did the same for Ainsley, her eyes dancing with laughter. Fox just rolled his eyes, but Ainsley leaned into the other woman's hold, needing a hug more than she'd thought she did.

"That's for the assist," Ainsley said with a wink. "Flour is dangerous."

"You don't see me when I bake usually. You see me with holiday baking, of course, but breads and other doughs? Flour everywhere." She patted her sides and smiled. "I just do a better job of hiding it before I walk out into the main room with everyone. You know, maybe I can get Loch to knock down that wall. I really want an open concept layout like in all those TV shows."

"Loch is a decent handyman, but I don't think he should be knocking down walls..." Ainsley smiled as she said it, but she could only imagine what Loch would do if he were asked to help. He'd do research, find someone to help him, and do it with his own hands just because that was who Loch was.

"True..." Barbara said, staring at the wall.

"What if it's load-bearing?" Fox asked, and the two women looked at him. "What? I know things."

"I don't know if it is, but there are posts and things you can put up. Our dining room and living room are open, but the kitchen can be so closed-off sometimes."

"Didn't you just say you liked keeping all the flour to yourself in the kitchen?" Ainsley asked.

Barbara just rolled her eyes. "You aren't letting me have any fun. I'm going to go out and tell Bob I want a new kitchen just to see how wide his eyes get." Her own eyes gleamed as she left, leaving Fox and Ainsley practically rolling on the floor.

"I want to be them when I grow up," Ainsley said.

"I know what you mean. I got pretty lucky in the parents' department. The fact they still love each other as much now as they did almost forty years ago says much about them. You know? I want that with Melody."

Ainsley's heart warmed. "I think you'll have it. You already have the foundation."

"Should I say something along the lines of you and Loch do, as well? Or are you going to kick me in the shin? Because I already have a bruise from Melody on my right one, so will you at least use the left? I'm fragile."

She tossed him a potato and glared. "Start peeling. And you know the rules, we don't talk about new relationships in the kitchen."

"You just made up that rule, so I don't know if I want to follow it."

"Remember, Fox, I'll be around for that baby. I'll be able to tell him or her all the little stories from when you were a kid that you might want to keep hidden."

"I have my parents for that, thank you very much. Did Melody tell you my mom sent her a *framed* photo of me naked on a bear-skin rug? Framed, Ainsley. Framed."

"I hope you were a baby and this wasn't a photo from last month. That would be weird."

He was the one who tossed the potato peel this time. "I hate you. But I love you, too. And I'm only going to say one thing. I know the world is coming at you two right now with a lot of crap that we'll all talk about later when Nate and Misty are napping or otherwise engaged, but I'm happy for you both. Loch needs someone, and while he's always had you because you're amazing, I'm glad he *really* has you now. And, Ainsley? I'm glad you have him, too. You make each other happy, and that's all I'll say." He paused. "For now."

Then he smiled and went back to work, leaving Ainsley wondering what would happen if it all changed. If what she and Loch were fighting for somehow slipped through their fingers, she might lose everything. Not just the man she loved, but everything. Loch was so ingrained in her life, she didn't know where she'd find the strength to knit herself and her life back together again. And if she lost Loch, despite his words, she could lose Misty and Loch's family, as well.

The family that had taken her in and made her feel like she was one of them.

She went back to cooking, and then later, ate her meal sitting between Loch and Misty, acting as if everything were fine. It wasn't, though. Because everyone around her was connected, was truly family. And Ainsley was one step away from that.

It might be different now, but it could all change.

And that worried her, maybe not as much as the danger lurking somewhere nearby, but enough that she couldn't properly taste the food everyone said was amazing.

She didn't want to *not* have Loch in her life, but she also knew she probably couldn't go back to being just friends.

He was her everything, despite her attempts for it not to be that way.

She let out a breath and smiled, though she knew Loch saw something in her eyes that worried him. She'd tell him her feelings. Later. After Riker had been caught and Loch was safe. For now, she'd smile and pretend that she wasn't worried about what would happen if it all ended. It didn't help anything to worry about something that might not happen at all.

But it was that *might* that would keep her up at night.

No matter how hard she tried to pretend it wouldn't.

Chapter 16

*L*och had a headache, and for some reason, even his tooth ached. He didn't have time for a cavity, but it seemed like his life wasn't going to slow down anytime soon. He stood in the parking lot, waiting to go in and pick up Misty from school. His work schedule was all messed up, and he was barely at the gym these days, doing his best to be there in-person for Misty and Ainsley for as many hours a day as possible.

Since Misty was only four, she didn't have full days at school, and there wasn't the normal drop-off line like there was for all the grades above her. It was going to suck next year when he had to wait in line like cattle to pick up his kid, but he'd work it out.

But staying in the parking lot meant he needed to deal with other parents, something he hated. He didn't actually hate all people, but he wasn't a huge people person, and dealing with other moms and dads was never his idea of a good time. Especially since, for some reason, this year, he was the only single dad of the bunch. Ainsley had told him it wasn't always this way, but he'd gotten the unlucky draw this year. It wasn't usually an issue, but there was one mom who was also single and *never* let him be.

He didn't want to be an asshole, but she damn well sure made him feel like one when he had to constantly put off her advances without letting their kids see what the hell was going on. There was a time and a place for crap like that, and in the school parking lot waiting for their little kids was not one of them. Plus, the woman wouldn't take no for an answer since he wasn't seeing anyone.

Or he *hadn't* been seeing anyone.

Well, then. Today might just be different, after all.

Tammy walked across the parking lot—or more like she prowled. Jesus, he did not have the time or patience for this today. He was sure she was a nice woman outside of his interactions with her, but she never listened to him and only looked at his muscles. Never his face. Yeah, he got it, he worked out, he owned a damn gym, but he didn't want to date her.

He was dating his best friend.

That thought made him smile despite the crap going on around him. Of course, it was the smile that Tammy saw when she stepped up next to him and, from the look in her eyes, he figured she thought it was for her. This wasn't going to be fun, not in the slightest.

"Loch. It's good to see you again."

"Tammy."

He checked his watch, not as discreetly as he might have in the past. Misty would be out any minute, and since he'd parked right at the front, she wouldn't have to walk past any cars to get to him. He kept an eye out, aware that Riker could be anywhere, considering what had happened to Ainsley the day before.

His blood boiled at the memory, and he had to calm his racing heart if he wanted to look like he wasn't a damn serial killer. Ainsley had slept over the night before, bringing her bag and everything else she might need with her. She'd slept in the guest room like she had in the past despite his protests since she'd said she wanted to talk to Misty first, and the night after a family dinner and the attack wasn't the time for it.

That meant it had been over a day since he'd held her in his arms and taken her to bed and he was done waiting. He didn't realize he would crave her as much as he did, and now that he'd had a taste, he knew he wouldn't ever stop wanting her.

"Loch? Did you hear me? They opened up that new restaurant on the other end of Main Street from your brother's place. Oh, it won't be as wonderful as Dare's since your family is so amazing, but do you want to try it out with me sometime? Just two friends…enjoying each other's company?"

Loch blinked, meeting Tammy's gaze for the first time. He hadn't heard what she'd said before, and he could have hit himself for that. He'd kept his attention on his thoughts and the door Misty would be coming out of, not on the woman in front of him asking him out…again.

Before, he'd been nice—apparently, too nice—but now he had an excuse that beat them all.

"Sorry, Tammy. If I try that place, I'll be going with Ainsley."

Tammy rolled her eyes. "Well, the two of you are cute as friends, but a man has needs, Loch."

There had to be a hole around big enough to bury him. Just put him out of his misery.

"I'm just fine, Tammy. I'm seeing someone."

Her eyes widened. "Oh. *Her*?" She blinked a few times. "Well, I guess I should say it's about time." She looked over her shoulder. "Have a good day."

Then she practically ran away, and Loch knew he hadn't handled that well. He wasn't the greatest in social situations, that was what Ainsley was good at in his opinion.

"Are you talking about Ainsley? Are you dating her, Daddy?"

Loch whirled as Misty threw herself into his arms, her smile wide, and her eyes even brighter than usual. He picked her up, holding her close, and looked around to see if anyone was near. He couldn't sense anything out of the ordinary, and no one seemed to be watching them, but he still held Misty close, annoyed with himself for once again getting distracted. Lives were on the line, and he was being an idiot. He wouldn't blame anyone for kicking him in the shin like Fox had talked about the night before.

"Hey, baby girl." He kissed the top of her head and carried her to his truck. "What were you saying?"

She rolled her eyes, and he narrowed his. When she gave him a sheepish look, he knew she was at least trying not to do it often but failing. Ainsley had said sarcastically that Misty would be fun as a teenager and Loch had a feeling they hadn't seen anything yet.

"Ainsley. You said you were dating. I know dating. That's when you go out and love each other. Ainsley, you go out with. You love her. But you need to take her out to a real place, Daddy. With real food. Not just at home. Ainsley's pretty, Daddy. I love her, too. So, yay!"

Loch buckled his kid into her booster seat as she rambled a mile a minute about her day at school. The snow that hadn't actually taken classes away, though some of the kids had wanted a snow day. Misty added in a few Ainsley topics along the way.

He cleared his throat as he tried to figure out what to say. He and Ainsley hadn't gotten around to talking about what they were going to tell Misty because while they wanted to be honest, it wasn't an easy conversation to have.

Misty, however, seemed to have ideas of her own.

"We'll talk about it when we get home." Misty was still too young to fully understand, and he didn't want to confuse her. It didn't help that he was already plenty confused himself.

"Okay, Daddy. Are we going to pick up Ainsley now? She's your girlfriend, right? Like Denny is Mary's boyfriend? He gave her a sticker, and she played with him at recess. You should give Ainsley a sticker."

Loch blinked and figured he'd have to have a talk about what exactly that meant in detail later. His kid was four, not twenty-four. There shouldn't be boyfriends or girlfriends at that age, and stickers shouldn't have anything to do with it.

"Mary is Denny's girlfriend?"

She nodded. "Yep." She popped the *p* in the word, and he shook his head. This kid, man. This kid.

"You don't have a boyfriend or a girlfriend, do you?" He wasn't sure he wanted to hear the answer since he was afraid she might say yes to both and end up with a sticker haul of her own he'd have to deal with.

She shook her head. "I can get my own stickers."

That made him laugh, and he leaned down to kiss her on top of her head. "That's my girl. Now, let's go pick up Ainsley, and we'll check out those stickers of yours." He paused. "Just know that if a boy or girl gives you stickers, you don't have to play with them at recess if you don't want to. Okay?"

"I know, Daddy. Just make sure you give Ainsley stickers or something she likes. Not so she'll play with you, but because they make her smile. She needs good things. We're her good things, too."

Out of the mouth of babes.

He kissed her again, then closed the door, heading to the front seat. He started his truck and pulled out of the parking lot, carefully avoiding Tammy's gaze on the way out. They made it to Ainsley's school soon after, and she grinned at them as she got into the truck. Though they hadn't had a snow day either, she hadn't had to stay late because of the weather, and today was one of the few days both schools let out at the same time. That meant he'd have time with both of his girls. Time where he could talk about stickers and dinner and other things that didn't bring up death and dark memories.

They'd had enough of that over the past few days and weeks, and somehow, the moment Ainsley jumped into the passenger seat, it felt like everything was normal, was exactly as it needed to be. There were still a few undercurrents in the air, the fact that he kept an extra-vigilant eye on his surroundings, worried about who could be watching, what could be waiting for him. The fact that his phone had a connection to the constant surveillance at his home and the gym. But he could pretend for a few moments that everything was fine.

Maybe starting a new relationship at the same time as everything going on wasn't the smartest thing in the world, but he wasn't going to change things now, not when this felt *right*.

He'd ask himself later why they hadn't done this before. But, then again, he could give himself that answer. The fact that Ainsley had been hurt the day before was answer enough, wasn't it?

"Hey there, you two," Ainsley said as she closed the door behind her. "Did you have a good day?"

"Yup," Misty said, popping that *p* again. "Ms. Tammy annoyed Daddy I think, but then he said he was dating and

I thought it was you, and he should give you stickers because you like happy. Can we have hot cocoa when we get home?"

Loch met Ainsley's wide eyes and snorted. "Hot cocoa we can do, but then we need to talk about this fascination you have with stickers."

"I like pretty things," Misty said, fluttering her eyelashes like one of the ponies in that show she liked to watch with all the colors and the stickers on their butts. Now, it made sense. Maybe.

"Should I ask?" Ainsley whispered.

He shook his head, then reached out and took her hand in his, tangling their fingers. "Later."

She looked down at their entwined hands, then back at Misty, who was grinning in the rearview mirror. When Ainsley looked back at him as he drove toward home, he gave her a smile, and she relaxed into the seat.

It was one step. Not the last, but it was something. There was no going back now. Then again, Loch wasn't sure there ever had been, not when he'd seen what he could have with Ainsley. He just hoped to hell he figured out what to do about Riker and the company before he lost it all.

Because he loved the woman next to him. Fucking loved her.

He just needed to figure out how to tell her that...while keeping her safe.

Chapter 17

*a*insley groaned as Loch's phone went off twenty minutes ahead of their alarm. He unwrapped himself from her, quickly rolling over and turning off the sound so it wouldn't echo throughout the house. Misty was probably still fast asleep since she didn't have to wake up early thanks to a school break day. A break that meant Ainsley didn't have to go to work either. She didn't understand why they had the day off right after a weekend without her having to go in for even a teacher workday, but she'd take the time off.

However, the phone ringing this early in the morning meant she wouldn't be able to go back to sleep anytime soon anyway.

She rolled over and looked at Loch's back, trailing her hand down his bare skin as she tried to wake up enough to understand what he was saying. She hoped it was just a normal call and not something serious, but she knew that wasn't going to be the case. Not when Riker was still out there, and God knew who else that was connected to Chris and that man.

Plus, with Melody pregnant and Kenzie trying, she was always afraid that a phone call this early in the morning would be about one of them. Thankfully, Misty was with them and not at the grandparents', meaning that was one less worry.

But from the gruff sound of Loch's voice and the tension in his shoulders, she knew that whatever the call was about, it wasn't good.

"I'll be there in ten minutes. No, that's fine. Thanks."

Loch hung up and turned to face her on the bed, his face screwed into a scowl she could see even in the dim light of the breaking dawn through the window.

"What is it?" She sat up, pulling the sheet over herself since she was cold without his body heat. She still wore his shirt and panties since Misty could come in at any moment because of a nightmare, and that meant Loch also wore shorts. Sleeping naked wasn't something you could do with kids in the house.

"Someone trashed my gym. Broke the windows, every fucking piece of equipment in there. Tore it all up with water and oil. Only thing they didn't do was set it on fire or get into my office since I added another set of locks on that with so much personal information stored there. But fuck it, Ainsley. It can't all be a coincidence. Especially since they somehow knew how to bypass my security. I didn't even get an alert on my phone."

She shook her head, reaching out to rub her hand down his arm, not knowing what else to do to comfort him. That place was his other home, his pride and joy. He'd put so much into it once he'd fully settled into Whiskey to be a father to Misty.

And now someone had ruined it all.

"Do you think it's Riker?"

"Unless I've pissed off a whole hell of a lot more people than I know about, it's the only thing that makes sense. I knew the man was living on the edge, but damn it, Ainsley, I don't know what he's playing at."

He leaned down and kissed her hard, then got up off the bed. He started pulling on clothes, and Ainsley got up, as well, pulling on hers from the day before. She'd shower and change into real clothes later, but she didn't like feeling as if she weren't prepared to leave if something happened. Not that anything would, but she was on edge, as well, as if waiting for the next shoe to drop. And she didn't like it.

"Are you heading down there, then?"

Loch nodded, tying up his shoes. "Got to meet with Renkle and Shannon again. They've got to be tired of meeting with me at this point."

"You're probably tired of them, as well." She went to him and wrapped her arms around his waist. For some reason, she was nervous about him going, even though it didn't make any sense. With the new security measures he'd added to the house, she and Misty would be fine, and she didn't think Riker was going to be prowling around the place he'd just destroyed with the cops around, but she still didn't like it.

She didn't like any of this.

"I am, but we're going to get to the bottom of this. He's making mistakes now, I know it. It's taken this long because we didn't put the pieces together, and I'm not a cop, remember? I'm just a guy with a family and the woman he loves in his arms. I don't know why Riker thinks this is the way to get what he wants, but he's wrong. Way fucking wrong."

Ainsley froze at his words, sure she was either still dreaming or not quite awake. "What did you just say?" she asked, her voice a whisper.

Loch stiffened, then looked down at her before moving to cup her face "Shit. I didn't mean to say that."

She was pretty sure her heart broke just then. Jagged pieces ripping and tearing until there was nothing left but a pile of ash and regrets.

"Oh."

He cursed again, then kissed her hard, his mouth a pressure point against hers. "No, that's not what I meant. I love you, Ainsley. I just didn't mean to tell you when I'm running out the door and dealing with the gym and who knows what else."

She took a step back, her heart beating so hard in her chest, she was afraid it would pop right out like in one of those cartoons Misty watched on Saturday mornings.

"Loch…"

His face shut down ever so slightly at the tone of her voice, and he gave her a tight nod. "I know it's fast and doesn't make any sense how I could love you so quickly, but the thing is, I've tried not loving you this way for so long, it's only natural that I feel this for you now that the blinders are off and we're finally where we should have been years ago. I'm sorry it took me so long, Ainsley. I'm sorry I was too stubborn to see what was right in front of me. I know you might not be ready to say the same words, and I get it. I was going to wait until we figured out who we are together outside of what's going on in the town. I mean, fuck, I haven't even taken you out on a real date. What kind of man am I?"

Ainsley threw her arms around his neck then, pressing her lips to his so he wouldn't talk himself out of loving her. She knew him and herself and they both could probably end up doing that if they talked in circles enough.

He wrapped his arms around her, tucking her close to him. They fit, and that was something she'd always known, even if she tried to forget that she wanted it to be true.

"I love you," she whispered against his lips. "I've loved you longer than I've known what you taste like on my lips. I thought you only saw me as your friend, and maybe that's the case, but, Loch? I love you so damn much. Misty, too."

He grinned then, tugging her close. "We'll move slower after this, I promise, but I like you in my bed, in my arms. In my life. After we stop Riker, we can talk about serious things, but I'm not letting you go, Ainsley. No matter what."

And when he kissed her again, she almost swooned in his arms. She'd never swooned before in her life but, apparently, today was starting out as a day for surprises.

She knew they had more to work out, more to deal with, but feelings couldn't be ignored. They hadn't even been together long enough for her mind to settle and yet… yet it worked. Because it was them. Because they were Loch and Ainsley. They'd been together for years, and yet… now it was different.

Now…now, she had hope.

LOCH HAD BEEN GONE for a couple of hours by the time Misty woke up, and Ainsley was making breakfast for the two of them. This wasn't the first time Ainsley had stayed over and made breakfast for Misty since she stayed in the guest room while Loch was out of town for work and she watched Misty overnight. It was always for work though, thankfully, and never for a date.

She winced. Nope, she didn't want to think about that. Loch had told her he'd never had another woman in that bed, only her, and that made her smile. She'd had another man in her bed, she hadn't been celibate before Loch, but she was territorial when it came to Loch, so she didn't mind being the only one when it came to him.

"I like that you're here and I don't have to wait for you to come over," Misty said before taking a bite of her pancake. Ainsley had gone overboard just a little with the chocolate chips, but it was her first morning alone with

Misty after staying over as Loch's girlfriend and she was still feeling her way. The situation was so different for her than it would have been for anyone else because of her relationship with Misty outside of her connection to Loch, but she *would* find her way.

"I like that I'm here, too."

"Are you going to stay here forever?"

Ainsley just smiled. "I have my own place." It was too soon to actually move in for real, and she knew it. She didn't want to rush things more than she already was and ruin what she had with the two most important people in her life. "But I'll be here like always. I'm just staying for a bit to help your dad." Sort of. They hadn't told Misty about what was going on in the town, but they had told her to be careful with strangers—like usual. Loch was good about things like that, and Ainsley was grateful.

"I like you here."

"I know. I like it here, too. But you like my place."

"Uh-huh."

Then the little girl just smiled and went back to her pancakes. Ainsley grinned and finished hers while making a grocery list. They were running out of certain things they'd need for the day, and she wanted to get it done. She often shopped for Loch, and he did for her, as well so it wasn't any different for her to do it today.

Except for the whole Riker thing.

She frowned and pulled out her phone, not knowing when Loch would be home. He'd been keeping her up-to-date and had called to talk to Misty earlier, but she knew he was dealing with the authorities, contractors, and who knew what else. Fox and Dare were down there, as well, their women helping out at Dare's inn since Melody's dance studio was located next to Loch's gym. The place was fine, but Melody was going to keep it closed until Loch knew what was going on. Both women had offered to come over to spend time with her, but Ainsley hadn't wanted to worry Misty.

Ainsley: *Hey, I need to go to the grocery store. Is it okay if I take Misty? Or should I wait for you to come home?*

Home.

She'd used the word *home* before when she stayed over because the context was easier, but now, it was different. Worrying over a word she used would give her a headache, though, so she pushed those thoughts out of her head.

Loch: *I'm going to be a few hours more. Sorry, babe. Go get what you need and put in on the card. Just be safe and check your surroundings. Can't live if you're constantly locked up...though I sort of want you to be.*

Ainsley grinned then and shook her head. She'd use his card even though she hated it. She didn't make much money as a high school teacher, and they both knew it. Loch made more and had invested wisely. So, for groceries and things having to do with Misty, she used the card he gave her even if she wasn't a huge fan of doing so.

Ainsley: *I'll be safe and take care of your girl. Just be safe too. Okay? Love you.*

It gave her a little thrill to write that last part, and she held back a giggle since Misty was watching her.

Loch: *Take care of both my girls. Love you too.*

And there went that thrill again.

"Want to go grocery shopping with me?" Ainsley asked, cleaning up their plates.

Misty bounced on the seat. "Yes!"

"Wash your hands and brush your teeth first."

"Okay, Ainsley." Then she was off like a rocket, and Ainsley just shook her head, putting the rest of the dishes in the dishwasher. She'd run it while they were gone, and after they came back, she'd start dinner since stew sounded amazing. It was one of the recipes she'd learned in her cooking class, and she hadn't tried it out on Loch yet. Hopefully, she wouldn't mess it up. But, hey, the pancakes had come out okay.

By the time the two of them were all bundled up and in Ainsley's car, headed to the store, both of them were a little hyper from the sugar in the pancakes and were singing to one of Misty's songs on the radio. Ainsley knew all the words since she was with her so often, and the two of them kept grinning and smiling…until a car pulled up right behind them, so close Ainsley couldn't even see its lights.

Ainsley turned down the music, hushing Misty when she complained, and sped up around the curve, trying to get to a place where this asshole could pass her and stop freaking her out. Only he wasn't moving away. Instead, he only got closer. Then he bumped her rear bumper, and Misty let out a scream.

Ainsley only barely held back one of her own as she

gripped the steering wheel, trying to stay on the road. But he bumped her again, and she slid off the gravel and into the farmland beside the road. They plowed through the grass, the sound deafening, but they didn't flip over. Instead, they came to a stop, the car shaking, and her pulse racing. There were no other cars around since they weren't on Main Street and it was still early on a weekday. She was grateful that they hadn't hit the embankment or one of the trees that lined the road.

Misty was crying behind her in her booster seat, and Ainsley shook as she put the car into park and tried to turn around to see if the little girl she loved was hurt.

"Misty? Are you okay?"

Misty nodded. "I want Daddy."

"Me, too." She turned to see if the other car had gone off the road, as well, the adrenaline in her system spiking to the point where she could barely think. But before she could take a good look around, she screamed and threw herself over Misty's legs, the only part of the little girl she could reach, as someone smashed the driver's side window into pieces. Then the door was being pulled open, and someone was reaching inside for Ainsley's seatbelt as they pulled on her hair with such force that her eyes watered.

As the man pulled her out of the car by her hair, her butt hitting the frozen ground with enough force to rattle her teeth, Ainsley kicked and screamed and tried to scratch at him, but he wore long sleeves and gloves.

She tried not to panic, but she knew it was no use when Misty was in danger, as well. She looked up as the man threw her to the ground so her head hit hard, but she was still able to look over at the car where another man was opening the back door and pulling Misty out.

Ainsley screamed again, this time kicking out when the man reached for her. He let out a grunt since she hit him in the knee, and then she scrambled to her feet, ignoring the blood on her hands from scraping them on the ground. She ran toward Misty, screaming her head off in hopes that *someone* might hear. But they were on the curve of Whiskey where there were no houses or businesses.

And these men had been watching. Waiting for her to get here.

Oh, God.

She didn't think either man thought she'd fight back, or that she'd have any skill, but Loch had taught her how to get safe and how to defend herself—at least as much as possible. With all of her strength, she threw herself at the man who had Misty by the hand and was trying to drag her out of the car rather than pick her up.

Thanks to gravity and the force of her body, Ainsley knocked the man down to the ground, both of them hitting the back of her car.

She rolled, but he rolled with her, pinning her to the ground. "Run!" she called out. "Misty, run!"

And the little girl did. Her little legs pumping as she ran away. That was what Loch had taught her to do. Run to a cop or to a family member. Run from strangers.

And, for some lucky, or maybe *un*lucky, reason, the other man didn't run after her. Instead, he came to Ainsley's side and tilted his head as he studied her. That was when she realized they were both wearing masks and the only thing she could see was their eyes.

"You're the one we need anyway," the one on top of her said, then he pulled back his fist and hit her.

Then she didn't see anything else.

Just darkness.

Again.

Chapter 18

*L*och rubbed the back of his head and got into his truck. He'd spent far too many hours this morning dealing with the aftermath of the destruction at his gym. He couldn't believe how much damage had been done in such a short period of time. While he wasn't going to have to start over from the ground up, it would be close.

The assholes had taken a sledgehammer to every piece of equipment in his place, and broken doors off their hinges to each of his private rooms except for his office. They'd shattered the floor-to-ceiling mirrors, torn down a few of the overhead lights, and had even damaged a few walls by using the sledgehammer on the drywall. They'd busted a pipe so water was everywhere, not to mention other fluids like oil and even gasoline. It was all far too deliberate and rage-filled.

So much anger, so much destruction. And for what? To piss Loch off? To try and scare him into giving Riker the company? It didn't make any sense to Loch, but it wasn't like he thought like the sociopath Riker likely was. Between Dennis—if the two were connected—attacking Ainsley when she was visiting her sister at the cemetery, breaking into Loch's place and trying to search for *something*, the note, the phone call, and now…this, Riker had clearly lost it, and Loch didn't think he would back down anytime soon.

But things still didn't click for Loch. The last time they'd spoken, it sounded like the police thought Riker had something to do with Dennis's death, but they weren't telling Loch either way. While he wanted to know everything, he didn't have the right to ask them about every detail. But still, his family was in danger, and he needed to know the facts. Only he wasn't sure the authorities had them all. At least not yet. Danger was piling up in Whiskey, something that didn't happen often, if ever, and Loch knew everybody was on edge, wanting to figure out how to stop it. The fact that Loch's past was the reason for all of it didn't sit well with him, but there was nothing he could do except tell the authorities everything he knew as well as try to help them find Riker.

Because, in Loch's mind, there was no doubt that the other man was connected to it all, even if he couldn't follow his former teammate's line of thought. Loch had feelers out with his old contacts to see if they knew where

Riker was staying, but so far, they'd come up as empty-handed as Loch had.

He'd keep looking, but right then, all he wanted to do was see if Ainsley was on her way home yet and go see his girls. He couldn't believe how quickly things had changed and yet, at the same time, it felt like nothing had. He and Ainsley had always been on this path despite ignoring the connection they had. They just hadn't seen what they could be to one another.

Or maybe Ainsley had always known, and he'd been the one to ignore it.

He hadn't been as dense as the rest of his family thought when it came to their curious glances over the years. He'd noticed when they were confused about Ainsley and him, looking between them as if they were missing something. Most of their friends thought they'd already slept together, but then again, Loch had done his best not to think about Ainsley that way until she'd been right in front of him, all angry and sexy as hell. Then, he'd gotten jealous. And now, well, the rest was history.

His phone rang then, pulling him out of his thoughts. Since he hadn't turned on the engine yet, it didn't go to his Bluetooth, so he picked up his phone to read the screen, frowning when it said *Unknown*.

Chills raced down his spine, and he answered, his voice gruff. "Yeah?"

"You should have just given me the company, Loch. You want nothing to do with it, we both know that. You left, remember? You abandoned the company and all we stand for and now you're living your perfect little life with your little brat and that bitch of yours. You should have given it to me, Loch. All you had to do was sign it over and no one would have gotten hurt. Now, you're a murderer, or at least the cops think that. Now you know your house isn't as safe as you thought. Now you know your work isn't the safe place you wanted it to be. Now you know you're never safe, Loch. You should have given it to me…but you still have time. Say the word, and all of this will be over. Just say the fucking word, Loch."

Then Riker hung up before Loch could say anything, and he blinked down at the phone, trying to remember and decipher everything the other man had said. If he had been smart, he would have recorded the conversation somehow, but he hadn't thought about it, and frankly, there hadn't been enough time, especially not knowing for sure who was on the other end of the line. Riker had talked without stopping like some villain from a damn movie with his diatribe and hadn't let Loch get a word in as Loch tried to make sense of the other man's words.

Riker had all but admitted that he'd murdered Dennis and tried to make it look like it was Loch, even though there hadn't been any real evidence or motive. And all of this for contacts and intel from a company with a good enough reputation that Riker could have probably gotten in with some major donors and bigwigs, making money and crossing lines for years before anyone even caught on that Jason's company wasn't the kind of place it had been before. With what Jason had left him, Loch knew that they were talking millions of dollars.

He shook his head, worried about what else Riker would do to get all that money and power. He'd already done so much, had pushed his men to break the law as he had with Chris, and from what Loch could see, he hadn't contacted the other man at all afterwards, probably cutting ties as soon as Chris got caught. It was insane.

Loch quickly called Detective Shannon, letting him know about the call since it was all he could do and, thankfully, the two detectives didn't want to talk to him again just then. They said they'd see what they could do with the number, but they weren't a high-tech station, and Loch bet Riker knew how to deal with disposable phones and other shit that would guarantee that no one would be able to trace the call. But they had to at least try because, at some point, Riker would make a mistake that would mean they could catch him. Because they had to, damn it. Loch's family wouldn't be safe otherwise.

Thinking of those he loved, he quickly called Ainsley, getting more nervous as the rings kept going and it went to voicemail. He tried again in case she was driving or dealing with Misty and couldn't talk, but it went to voicemail another two times. He put his phone in the drink holder and started his truck, practically peeling out of the parking lot of his gym as he went the back way to his place. If Ainsley had gone to the grocery store, this would be the way she'd go; it was the quickest. And except for one small part, it was completely lined with homes and businesses. It should be safe. *Whiskey* was supposed to be safe.

Loch called Fox, then Dare, asking if they'd heard from Ainsley, both saying they hadn't but would ask the rest of the family for him and would get back to him before they started looking, as well. That was his family, always on his side, protecting what was there even if they were all scared as fuck about what was happening.

He took the curve toward his place, then slammed on his brakes as he saw a very familiar little girl with wide eyes and tears streaming down her face, standing between two strangers on the side of the road, a sedan he didn't recognize pulled over near them.

He pulled in behind them, then threw his door open, running toward the couple and his daughter.

"Misty!"

"Daddy!"

She ran past the couple, who didn't stop her. Staying on the side of the road rather than on it, he ran to her as well, picking her up as she jumped toward him and crushing her to his chest.

"Baby, what's wrong? Why are you out here? What's going on?" He was rambling, asking too many questions for a four-year-old to answer at once, but he was goddamn shaking. Where was Ainsley? He didn't ask that, too scared to even voice it.

"They took Ainsley, Daddy!" Misty was screaming now, her little body shaking so much in his hold he was afraid she was going into shock. He patted her back, rocking her back and forth as he tried to calm both of them down. His heart was beating so fast, he almost forgot all of his training over the years. He could barely think straight.

"What?"

"Sir?" the woman asked, her voice shaking, as well. She had to be a tourist or just driving through since he didn't recognize her. "We saw her running on the side of the road, and we pulled over. She started crying and screaming and wouldn't come close, and we understood that she was scared of us, too. So, we called the police. They should be here soon. She didn't say a word to us, so we don't know who she's talking about or who Ainsley is or even what happened, but you have a smart little girl there. She knew what to do with strangers. And we're sorry if we scared her, but we didn't want her to be alone, even if she was just standing near us and not coming close."

Loch soothed his little girl, who had quieted down to a whimper now as sirens filled the air, getting closer. He was damn tired of that noise, especially since it always seemed to do with him lately, but he wanted them to check out Misty. And fuck, he needed to find Ainsley.

"Thank you," Loch said, his voice a growl. He knew he was a bit big and scary, but he had his daughter in his arms, and the love of his life was out there *somewhere*. "Thank you for doing all you did."

He didn't know what else to say while the other couple introduced themselves and started talking to fill the silence as they waited for the cops and the ambulance to come. He was pretty sure they were the same paramedics from the graveyard and that just reminded Loch of Ainsley.

Where was she?

And how the fuck was he going to find her?

Because he *knew* Riker had her. After that phone call, it made the most sense. He needed to find her. Needed to save her. Because if he lost Ainsley after just finding her, he'd never forgive himself. Riker would regret even coming near what was Loch's.

But he might only regret it for a little while because if Loch had his way, the other man wouldn't be breathing for long.

Loch needed to find Ainsley.

No matter what.

Chapter 19

*A*insley coughed up water as Riker removed the towel from her face. He'd introduced himself to her, along with another man named Jeff when they'd first gotten to the empty farmhouse. She'd only known it was abandoned because the place looked ready to fall down around them, and the amount of dust on every surface was enough to make her eyes water.

Of course, since Riker and his man had been pouring water over her face through a towel, her eyes were watering now for a whole different reason.

Riker slapped her then, her eyes stinging, and her face red and battered. She knew she'd be a mess when she got out of here, bruised and maybe even broken.

But she *would* get out of here.

She wouldn't let Riker win.

Loch wouldn't let Riker win.

And she would do her damnedest to get out of here, somehow, so Loch wouldn't have to blame himself for any of this. Ainsley didn't know why they were torturing her. She had nothing to do with Loch's past or with the company. She might be Loch's best friend, but she only knew the basics of what he'd told her over the years and just recently.

Riker and Jeff seemed to want to hurt her to make Loch hurt when he found her. She hated Riker even more for what he was doing to her, not only because it hurt—because it did—but because it was a cruel and round-about way of hurting Loch. They wanted to hurt him from the inside, to use guilt and recrimination to make the man she loved hate himself. And all she wanted to do was get out of these ropes and find a way to scratch Riker's eyes out.

Unfortunately, she wasn't strong enough for that, but she could at least keep trying to escape.

She was afraid they were telling her too much about their plans to keep her alive at this point, and she was doing her best to swallow down the bile in her throat that rose just thinking about it. They weren't going to keep her alive. They were going to make her hurt, then they were going to kill her. Either they'd leave her body where Loch could find it, or they'd find a way to make the police think it was him.

Or…they'd wait to kill her in front of him.

Because these men were not sane. That was clear. They were the evilest of the evil, and she hated them.

She just hoped to God that Misty had gotten somewhere safe.

Tears once again filled her eyes as she thought of that little girl. She couldn't believe she hadn't been strong enough to see her to safety. She'd done everything she could, but she didn't know if it had been enough.

"Had enough?" Riker growled. She lay still, her hands fisting behind her back in their rope bonds. He leaned over her, his face no longer in its mask. Jeff and Riker had both stripped them off when they reached the house, not caring that she saw their faces. They hadn't cared that they talked about their plans for Loch in front of her either.

She was certain she would die today if she didn't save herself, if she didn't stay alive long enough for Loch to find her. That much she knew, and though she was scared beyond measure, she knew if she didn't make a plan, they'd take away any hope she still had.

And all she'd had before this was hope.

She couldn't stop now.

When she didn't answer, Riker slapped her again, and she closed her eyes, tears falling down her cheeks at the sting. Her jaw ached, and she was afraid she'd bitten her tongue. She didn't want to bleed, didn't want to give this man the satisfaction.

"Loch should have done the right thing in the first place. But he didn't listen." Riker started pacing around the small room as Jeff left the building. She didn't know what he was doing, but she figured it wasn't something that would help her escape. As Riker talked, she tried to work on her ropes behind her body, aware that as long as he faced the wall like he currently did, he'd be able to see her face, as ragged and beaten as it was, but wouldn't be able to see her hands. "

Riker growled and continued. "The courts took everything from me. They took the company because Jason was a fucking idiot and either didn't update his will enough or didn't want to let go of his dreams for his prize boy. What the hell did Loch ever do for him, huh? He was *nothing*. Jason saw what he wanted to see, but he didn't see the real man. He didn't see that Loch didn't have any balls. Loch left us, didn't take the risks that were needed to make the company work. But I did. I still do. But when Loch sees what I can take from him, he'll give me the company, and I'll do what Jason and Loch never could. I'll make it great again. I'll make us the best."

He had lost his damn mind, but it didn't matter what Ainsley thought of him. Because he had the upper hand. And unless she found a way out of this, he was going to kill her. But she knew she wasn't strong enough unless she ran or snuck away.

No number of weapons or self-defense classes were going to keep her alive then—just luck and determination.

Ainsley didn't say anything. She didn't need to, not when the man liked to hear himself talk rather than listen to anything sane.

"We need the contacts the company has, the ones that Jason kept to himself. We need the confidential data, the stuff the bastards never allowed me to see. Loch will have all of it now. Once we have it, Loch can go on his merry way. We won't bother him."

A lie.

They both knew it, but Riker kept going, the vein on his temple bulging.

"The company should have been mine. Even as Jason started to pull back, his age getting the best of him, you see, I was the one making decisions. We killed who we needed to, never held back because we were too scared to make the choices that needed to be made. Holding back because you think you should have a set of morals wastes time. People get killed, money gets lost. But I don't make those bad choices. I never did. And when Jason didn't see that..." Riker shrugged. "Well, Jason didn't need to be around anymore. But the asshole didn't give me the company. He gave it to his *favorite*."

Riker spat the word, and Ainsley swallowed hard. This man, with his petulant complaints as if he were a child not given the toy he wanted, had killed Loch's mentor, too? Loch had wondered if Jason died from natural causes, but the way Riker had just casually thrown that fact out there just cemented the idea that she wasn't getting out of this farmhouse alive unless she forced her way out.

Ainsley didn't want to die today.

She wanted her happily ever after, the one she'd never thought possible. She wanted to keep teaching, wanted to watch those children grow into amazing, capable adults. She wanted to finish cooking classes with Fox. She wanted to learn to dance with Melody. She wanted to see Kenzie bloom into the mother she was meant to be. She wanted Dare to expand his business and be an amazing father twice over. She wanted to see Tabby have her twins and meet those babies. She wanted Tabby's husband to come to Whiskey and be enveloped by the family. She wanted to see her mother again and tell her that she loved her. She wanted to see Katie's grave again. She wanted to hold Misty and watch her grow up. She wanted to be with the man she loved and become his wife when the time came.

She wanted it all.

But she wasn't going to get any of it if she didn't find a way to get out of her ropes and get away from Riker and Jeff.

Riker left her for a moment, pacing along the wall on the other side of the room as Jeff walked in. The two started talking to one another, ignoring her. Though Ainsley knew if she moved too much in any direction, they would notice. They were as alert as Loch was, and Loch noticed everything, even if he thought himself distracted at times.

With her eyes on them, Ainsley slowly worked the rope behind her back. They'd tied her up tightly, but Loch had also taught her how to get out of a few kinds of knots. He'd tied her up a few times during their self-defense lessons, and though she'd been having inappropriate thoughts the entire time, she'd learned a few tricks. Never once, however, did she think she'd have to actually use them.

She'd have to kiss that man over and over again in

thanks when she got out of this. Not *if*, because she wasn't going to stop fighting, no matter what.

It took patience, and she had to stop a couple of times when Riker came back over to goad her again with slaps and taunting scrapes of his knife down her cheek, but she didn't cry out, didn't let him know that she was almost out of her bonds. But when he turned his back for the fourth time, the ropes fell away, now clasped in her palms rather than tied around her wrists.

She wouldn't die.

Not today.

The relief at knowing she was one step closer to freedom didn't come. Instead, her stomach rolled, and she was afraid she might throw up. Getting out of her ropes had been the easy part. Getting out of the house without getting seriously hurt or dying would be much harder.

But when Jeff said he was going out to the truck to check on something, Ainsley knew this was her only chance. She could *maybe* get away from one of them. But two? She didn't stand a chance—no matter how much desperation gave her an edge.

Riker came closer to her then, hovering over her like the snake he was. "We called Loch, and yet...he didn't offer us the company or the contacts. Seems he doesn't care about you, after all."

She ignored his words, knowing he was only taunting her. Loch would do anything to save those he loved, and that scared her. Because she didn't want anyone else getting hurt because of her, she didn't want *Loch* hurt because of her. So, she'd find a way to get to him rather than the other way around.

At least, she hoped.

When Riker put his hand over her mouth, she knew this was her chance. Either she let whatever happened to her happen, or she found a way to get out.

So, she bit him on the finger.

Hard.

Riker screamed and cursed, staggering back a few steps in the opposite direction, holding his bloody hand to his chest. Ainsley took those few seconds to leap up from her chair and run toward the door. She must have shocked him because he didn't move for a heartbeat. She didn't know if Jeff was right outside the front door or not, but she didn't have a choice. She had to take a chance. She either tried to make a break for it, or she didn't. Ever.

Riker met her at the door, pulling at her hair as he had in her car. She screamed, ducking out of the way this time because she had the room. When her eyes caught on something that glinted in the low light of the bare bulbs above them, she jumped for it, her hands landing on the hilt of a small knife.

She really didn't know what to do with a weapon, she wasn't trained in them and could likely hurt herself more than Riker, but she was out of options.

Riker lunged at her, an expression of triumph on his face. He obviously knew she wasn't good with a blade, but that didn't mean she couldn't try. So, she thrust her arm out, the knife pointed toward Riker. When she heard the sickening sound of something sharp going into a piece of meat, like when she stabbed a raw roast, she almost gagged.

She looked down at where she'd embedded the knife deep into Riker's side and then looked back up at his face. He looked like he couldn't quite believe what she'd done. She couldn't either for that matter. But his slight hesitation when he groaned in pain and clutched his side gave her all the time she needed. She was out the door in the next instant, running through the forest with the snow crunching under her shoes. She wasn't wearing a jacket, they'd taken that off her in order to mess with her in the chair, and the bitter wind slapped at her skin, sinking into her bones. Freezing the water still on her clothing and in her hair.

But she ignored it all.

If she kept moving, she'd find her away to a road and then to someone who could help her. She couldn't stop, couldn't think about what she'd done or what could still come at her. She just had to get to someone, had to get to Loch.

She turned a corner, getting near a clearing where she could hear the trickle of the almost frozen creek she knew surrounded Whiskey, when something slammed into her back. She hit the ice-cold ground with a thud, dirt and branches digging into her palms, leaving a bloody trail in their wake as she rolled to her back.

Jeff was on top of her, his hands around her throat and a wild gleam in his eyes. She panicked, clawing at his fingers, trying to pull him free so she could breathe. She broke a nail, the jagged edge cutting into his skin, but he still didn't pull away. Instead, he squeezed harder.

She blinked, her vision going dark at the edges as she fought for breath. She reached around for something, *anything* to try and get free. She couldn't die, not after all she'd done to escape. She was *so* close. If she could have made it past the creek, she would have been near people who could help.

Her hands slid over the dirt, shaking as she tried to find something. Anything to use as a weapon. When her fingers closed over a pointed rock, she pulled it up and slammed it into Jeff's head with all of her remaining strength. She didn't even think about what she was doing. It was all instinct, she just hoped to hell it was enough to let her have even a fraction of a second of breath.

Jeff blinked at her, blood pouring down from his temple, then his hold slackened, and he fell on top of her, his head slamming into the ground beside her face.

She scrambled from beneath him, her whole body shaking as she coughed, gasping for breath. She kept moving, though, knowing Riker could be close, and Jeff could wake up at any moment. She just needed to get help, then she'd be free. Then she'd be okay.

And if she kept telling herself that, she might truly believe it.

She made it to the creek edge, knowing she was going to have to cross it, the idea of hypothermia on her mind, but she didn't care. She had no choice. She took one step into the icy water, her bloody hand over her mouth so she wouldn't cry out. Then, someone tugged on her arm, pulling her back and down into the water. Her butt slammed into the rocky bed, and she splashed around, trying to get free.

Riker growled over her, doing his best to push her under. Blood seeped from his wound and into the water around them, mixing with her own.

He grinned at her, a manic gleam in his eyes that told her that this was it.

She hadn't been strong enough.

But she'd tried.

And, in the end, she could cling to that.

"Stop!" she screamed. "Let me go!" She just hoped someone would be near enough to hear her, that someone would be able to help.

Riker slammed her back into the creek. "Shut up, bitch." Then he dunked her head under the frigid water, and she thrashed, trying to break free.

He pulled her up again, and she gasped for breath, trying to roll away, but she couldn't get loose, couldn't tug herself free.

"It's over, Ainsley. Just give up. There's no point in fighting. There never was."

And as the darkness settled in, as she knew her end was coming, she thought she heard Loch's voice, thought she heard his shout. But that couldn't be, because this was the end.

She'd lost.

But she'd fought.

She'd tried.

And now she would see Katie again, even if it was too soon.

Loch's voice echoed in her head again, and she wondered what he could be saying as she was almost ready to say goodbye.

Because he couldn't be here. No one was. She was alone except for an unconscious Jeff…and Riker.

Alone.

And gone.

Chapter 20

*L*och slammed his fist into Riker's face as he tugged the other man off Ainsley's body. He hoped to hell that he'd been quick enough, that he and his brothers had found the place in time.

It had been Fox who found the abandoned farmhouse. Because the place wasn't within Whiskey lines, the town hadn't known that someone had called in to complain about a light being on at the old farm that shouldn't have anyone in it. He and his brothers had told the police about it, and the authorities were on their way, but Loch and his brothers had been closer. They'd come first, knowing they'd get yelled at, but Loch didn't give a shit. He'd needed to make sure Ainsley was okay, needed to make sure she was safe.

Dare was in the water, tugging Ainsley up and out of the creek as Fox tried to get a signal to tell the police exactly where they were since they were off the trail from the house. He couldn't tell if Ainsley was moving, couldn't see if she was even breathing, but he was the only one of his brothers who could take down Riker without killing him, and he didn't want the other man to die. He wanted him to live, rotting in a cell, feeling pain for the rest of his life.

"You fucking bastard," Riker spat, blood dripping down his chin and from his side. Someone, probably Ainsley, had stabbed the asshole, and Loch was proud of her—and scared shitless at the same time. What exactly had this man done to her when Loch had been too far away, unable to help her because he hadn't been fast enough?

Loch swallowed down the bile in his throat and swung out, trying to subdue Riker. He wanted the man out of the way and not able to hurt anyone else he loved until the cops arrived. He'd even take their help right then, anything so he could get Ainsley into his arms and out of the way of Riker's insane plans—whatever the hell those were.

When he and his brothers had gotten to the farmhouse, he'd almost thrown up. There had been water everywhere, and wet towels that he had a feeling had gone over Ainsley's face when they'd fucking *waterboarded* her. There had been blood on the floor, and her jacket ripped to shreds near some tattered rope. He'd followed her trail, including some of what had to be hers or Riker's blood until they found Jeff's unconscious body. Loch had quickly used the zip ties he'd brought with him to keep the man down, then had kept going to the creek where he'd found Riker trying to drown Ainsley.

The fucker had almost done it, too.

But from the way Ainsley was coughing in Dare's arms to the right of Loch, she was breathing.

He let that relief slide over him as he growled low, ducking out of the way of Riker's fist. "We're done, Riker. You're done. You lost. This is over. Do you get it? You're unarmed, and there are three of us to one of you. Jeff's down for the count, and I don't want to kill you, but if you come near me and mine, I will. Do you get me? It's over. Don't lose your life because you're a selfish asshole."

"Four," Ainsley coughed, but Loch didn't look over at her, just kept his eyes on Riker. "There are four of us. Fuck. You. Riker."

Then Loch grinned, his love for the woman to his right so fierce, he almost asked her to marry him right then. Because, why the hell not? Nothing else made sense today. Not even a little bit.

Riker screamed and turned toward Ainsley, and Loch was suddenly done. He tackled the other man to the ground, hitting him over and over in the face until he knew Riker's nose was broken and the other man was finally unconscious—not dead, but close enough that he knew it would take a while for the bastard to heal.

Good.

Then he tied him up as the authorities slid through the trees, Shannon and Renkle leading the way. They looked at the five of them, brows raised, then came to help. Loch was already up and away from Riker, leaving the other man to the police and whoever else wanted jurisdiction since they weren't technically in Whiskey. Fox and Dare surrounded him as he held Ainsley close, kissing her cold lips and hoping to hell she was okay.

"Baby," he whispered.

"I'm okay," she said, her whole body shaking, her lips blue. "I'm okay." She repeated it over and over again, and Fox called out for the paramedics to come over. Loch knew the others were saying things, asking questions, but right then, he could only focus on the woman in his arms.

"Is Misty...?" Ainsley coughed before she could finish her question, and he knew he'd have to let her go soon, but he wanted to keep her in his arms and warm for as long as possible.

"She's fine. Safe. Scared, but safe. You saved her, Ainsley. You saved her." He kissed her again. "And you saved yourself." He knew she'd fought for her life, and though he'd been the one to end things with Riker, he knew he would have been too late if she hadn't fought as hard as she did.

"I love you," he whispered.

"I know." She leaned into him, and he shook her a bit to make sure she didn't go to sleep as the paramedics came closer, getting out their equipment as they started to take her vitals, even with her still in his arms.

"You hated that line in that movie," he growled, trying to keep her smiling, even if it didn't reach her eyes.

"Well, I get it now," she said, her voice a little drowsy,

so he hugged her tighter as the paramedics wrapped a blanket around her shoulders. Dare was wearing one as well since he'd gone into the water, but his brother was on the phone with Kenzie, giving the family the updates he could.

"Seriously?" he asked, moving out of the way slightly so the EMTs could work on her bloody hands. He held back a growl at the sight of them, knowing her injuries could have been far worse...though he didn't know the full extent of them yet.

She looked up at him, a light in her eyes he was afraid he'd never see again. "Okay, fine. I love you."

"I'll take that."

Then he held her close as everyone started talking at once, doing what they needed to for the scene, for Ainsley's health, and even for Loch's knuckles. He knew there would be more questions to come, more answers they needed that he might not have, but for now, he just held Ainsley close to him, knowing his brothers had his back like always. There would be more time to talk later.

There will be more time, he repeated to himself.

More time because Ainsley had fought to save her life, and Loch and his brothers had been just fast enough for an outcome that didn't mean more death.

And in the end, that had to count for something.

Chapter 21

*T*wo weeks later, Ainsley lay in Loch's bed, Misty cuddled up against her side, deep in sleep after their second story time of the night. Loch was helping Dare out behind the bar tonight since Ainsley had kicked him out of the house, his hovering adorably sweet but a bit overwhelming after a while.

Her hands were healed, as were the other cuts and bruises she'd gotten from the ordeal. She'd lost a couple of clumps of hair but had added a few new layers to her hairstyle a few days after she got home to camouflage it. Her face had taken the longest time to heal, and she knew that every time Loch looked at her, he got angry and blamed himself. But he never said anything. Instead, he left gentle kisses on her bruises and held her hand.

He was always touching her, always making sure she felt loved and cared for.

They were doing the same with Misty, making sure the little girl knew that Ainsley and Loch weren't going anywhere, that they loved her and were going to take care of her.

Misty had nightmares, but they were getting better each night. Ainsley, much the same. It helped that the three of them also went to a therapist, Ainsley and Loch now going alone, as a family, and as a couple. It was the same therapist that Melody, Fox, Kenzie, and Dare had used after their issues and were still seeing. At some point, maybe the Collins family could get a group discount, but Ainsley never wanted to think too hard about that.

She hadn't gone back to work, her sub taking over with perfect ease. She'd go back soon, though everyone said she could have the semester off if she needed time. They were being so generous with her, her students even sending letters and emails to make sure she knew they were keeping up with their lessons and were thinking about her.

She would go back, probably on Monday, healed and ready to try and be normal again. It wasn't that she would have lasting scars on her body, but her soul ached. She'd thought she would die, had thought she'd never hear Loch's voice again except for what she'd thought had been her imagination. Instead, it had actually been him screaming for her as he saved her life.

He'd told her that she saved herself, and she truly believed that she had partly saved herself when she was able to get away from Riker the first time and from Jeff the second. But Loch had been the one to save her in the end.

When Loch told her that she'd saved him, as well, she hadn't believed him, but then he'd said that she was his and, without her, he'd have been lost.

The two of them were best friends. They were lovers. And they were *in* love. With Misty, they were a family. It was as if they had always been one, even if she knew that others might think they were moving too fast. They weren't. They were moving at their own pace, and that was all that mattered. They weren't confusing Misty, and they were staying true to themselves.

That was why she hadn't moved out yet, and knowing Loch, she probably never would. It was as if she had always been there, and once she and Loch had finally opened up to one another, everything just clicked into place.

She didn't know what would happen next, though she had a small plan she hoped would work out. Yes, everything was too soon for others, but she and Loch weren't everybody else. Their bond had been forged when they were friends, had settled into place over the years of being close and being who they were, and had been tested and found stronger than ever when Riker had tried to ruin their lives.

Now, Riker, Chris, and Jeff were being tried for countless crimes, Dennis had been laid to rest, surrounded by those who had known him and would miss him. Whiskey was coming back to itself, putting its unraveled and undone recent past behind it.

And Ainsley could smile with this little girl in her arms and in her heart.

It counted.

"There my girls are," Loch whispered. "She's out, isn't she?"

Ainsley smiled and looked up at the sound of his voice, her breath catching. Yes, it still caught at the sight of him, she couldn't help it. He was her Loch, and no matter how many times they were together, it always felt like the first and the thousandth time all at once.

"Like a light. We went through two stories, and I didn't want to wake her if I had to move her."

"You shouldn't be picking her up anyway. Not yet."

She rolled her eyes. "Loch. I'm fine."

"Sure." She knew he didn't believe her, but that was okay. She'd scared him just as much, if not more than she'd scared herself. And if he had to act like a big, growly bear for a bit longer, she'd let him. And when and if it got to be too much, she'd kick his ass like always. It was how they worked, even when they were only friends.

Not that there was anything *only* when it came to Loch.

Loch pressed a soft kiss to her lips, then picked up Misty and carried her to her bedroom where he presumably tucked her in. Ainsley settled herself against her pillows, waiting for him to come back and tuck her in because he would. He was getting sweet on her, and she kind of liked it, even when he growled while doing it.

When he came back in, he kissed her again, then laid next to her on one side, his head resting in his hand.

"What?" she asked when he just stared at her without saying anything.

He kissed her shoulder. "You're going to marry me."

She blinked, her heart racing even as she kept her voice calm and her face devoid of emotion. "Oh, good, I'm glad we're getting over the caveman part of this relationship."

He snorted, then started playing with the edge of her tank. "Seriously, it's going to happen."

"So you say."

"I say you're going to marry me. It doesn't matter that it's only been a short while since we've called each other what we are together now. The timing is right. So, yeah, you're going to marry me."

He kept saying those words in that confident way of his, and it was all she could do to not jump on the bed in glee. Instead, she just gave him a wry look and played.

Because he was still her best friend, and playing around was part of the fun.

"Fine, I'll marry you, but only because I want Fox and Dare as my brothers and Tabby is already taken."

"I hate you, and I love you," he growled, even as he moved to settle over her, taking her lips with his. She leaned into him, missing his touch, but he'd been *very* careful not to touch her in that way since the incident. She didn't think he would tonight either, not until he knew she was safe and healthy. She didn't mind because she knew she'd have forever with him, even if she hadn't thought she'd have a forever at all.

"I know, same here." She grinned up at him, her body

shaking because hell, he was hot, and she couldn't believe they were actually talking about this right now and right then. "Oh, can you get my bag?"

"Seriously?"

"Yes, seriously. I need to get something."

He sighed and then rolled off her, careful not to put any weight on her as he grabbed her bag from the chair next to the window. "Here. What's so important in that massive purse of yours?"

She just smiled and dug around until she found what she was looking for. Her hands shook, and she was so damn scared, but then again, nothing worth having came without a cost. Nerves were just part of it. She pulled out the small box she'd hidden in her bag the day before and held it out to him.

"Beat you. I win." At least, she hoped she did.

He looked down at the ring in the box and blinked up at her, his mouth open like he had no idea what to say. Then again, she didn't get to surprise him often. He always seemed to know everything, but today, that wasn't going to happen.

"What? I wanted to ask you. I'd get down on one knee, but you haven't let me out of bed in two weeks."

"You…you're asking me to marry you? With a ring? I have a ring in the drawer next to you, but I was going to wait until you were ready."

She swallowed hard. "I'm ready now. So are you, hence the whole conversation we just had about you deciding I was going to marry you instead of the whole, you know, asking thing. But it's us. So, why don't we just do what we want and do it *how* we want?"

Her heart practically beat out of her chest as she waited for his answer. But when he didn't say anything, she was afraid she'd screwed up. What if he had other plans? What if the idea of a ring and an actual answer was too much for him and she'd ruined it all by going too fast even if they said it wasn't?

Then he leaned down and kissed her on the nose, then the cheeks, then the lips, before taking the box from her hands and sliding the ring onto his finger. It wasn't a wedding band, but a handcrafted one that was made of white gold and had carvings in the side. She'd gotten it at a small shop in Whiskey, one that catered to the beautiful and unique, something she always thought Loch was, though she didn't dare call him that to his face. Tears filled her eyes, but he didn't kiss her again, didn't say anything as he opened the drawer next to her and pulled out a little box that looked similar to hers.

Of course, he'd gone to the same place she had.

That's why they were best friends.

He slid the three-stone ring onto her finger, and she studied the tiny pearls on the side, so little, she didn't know how he'd found something so perfect. He'd found the ring that was just for her, just as unique as his.

Just as beautiful.

"God, I love you. And, yes, I'll marry you, but if anyone asks, I was the one to ask you."

"Nope, I'm telling everyone you swooned."

And then he kissed her, and she knew everything was exactly as it needed to be. Perfect. Theirs. With a forever she hadn't seen coming.

Epilogue

Later.

$\mathscr{L}$och leaned back in his lawn chair, watching his family hang out in his parents' backyard, a grin on his face that he didn't realize he had until Ainsley looked over at him, grinning right back. He gave her a wink, and she went back to talking with her mom, who sat on the other side of her.

It had been a long year, but everything that had happened in that year hadn't been painful, not like the year prior with his family. Instead, it had been…peaceful. So much had happened after Riker and his cronies had gone to jail, and yet none of it had involved the police or people out to hurt Loch's family.

Instead, there had been change, yet all for the better.

"Daddy! Mommy! Look!"

Both Loch and Ainsley looked over at Misty, who stood near Tabby and Alex. His sister and her husband were sitting on a large blanket, their twins Sebastian and Aria scooting around, laughing as Misty twirled in her spring dress.

The fact that she'd called Ainsley *Mommy* wasn't lost on any of them, nor was it the first time she'd done it.

Misty had given Loch away to Ainsley and had given Ainsley away to Loch at their wedding just a couple of months before, and ever since then, she'd called his wife "Mommy" and "Mom." Every time she did, though, it hit Loch like an arrow to the heart, making him feel like he'd saved the world.

Ainsley smiled widely at him, and so did her own mother, who had finally come to a Collins family event. The two were working on their relationship, and he knew that he'd do whatever it took to keep his wife happy. Ainsley's mom was a good woman, and she had sacrificed a lot of herself to raise her kids. And when things had all come falling down around her, she'd tried to be strong for Ainsley. In the end, it had taken both of them to figure out what worked for their relationship.

Ainsley wanted her mother to know Misty, to be another grandmother in his little girl's life, as well as a grandmother to the baby currently growing in Ainsley's womb. They were only three months pregnant and hadn't announced it yet. They wouldn't until next month when they told Misty, but he couldn't help the proud, caveman-like grin spreading over his face.

"I like when the babies laugh," Nate said from Fox and Melody's blanket near Tabby and Alex, pulling Loch from his thoughts. "I can't get CP to laugh like that." He looked down at his cousin and frowned. "She doesn't laugh like they do."

Melody grinned and held her daughter close. "Caitlyn Pearl is just a little younger than the twins. She'll be laughing like them any day now. I love their giggles."

Fox smiled and kissed his wife's head. "Soon, your new baby brother and sister are going to be around, so you can start trying to make them laugh, as well."

Nate nodded. "I'm getting *two* at the same time, but not like Aunt Tabby and Uncle Alex. My brother and sister won't be twins, won't even be related, but I'm still going to call them brother and sister."

Dare and Kenzie were expecting a boy, and Dare's ex, Nate's mom, was expecting a little girl the same month as they were. Considering the other couple was at the Collins family barbeque, as well, seated right next to Dare and Kenzie as they watched over Nate, Loch figured the family, extended and complicated as it was, was making it work. Even Dare's former partner's widow was at the house, her daughter in tow as she melded into the family as if she'd always been a part of it.

Somehow, the family had grown to include more than only the Collinses. Dare had his whole brood, including family friends that were now part of his extended family, even if it was only through friendship. Melody's grandmother sat next to Loch's parents, laughing at some story she was telling them about the old days in Vegas, but keeping it rated PG for the kids in the yard.

Everything had changed since his brothers and sister had started finding their spouses, and yet it was all for the better. In the past year, Dare and Kenzie's inn had grown, same with the bar and restaurant, with the idea of expanding into other small towns on the horizon. Melody's dance studio was rocking with Melody back from maternity leave and her new assistant from her old school a wonderful addition. Fox and Ms. Pearl were in the middle of writing a *book* about her life, something he'd never thought his little brother would do. Ainsley was working full-time again, though things were going to change when the baby came, but Loch would make it work so she could keep her job the way she'd always wanted. He was going to be the one staying home with the baby and Misty. He would hire an additional manager to take care of the gym.

He had more than enough money now thanks to the sale of the company and what Jason had left him. Loch and Ainsley had decided to use the money to build their future for their children rather than toss it away because it held too much grief. They'd use it for good rather than whatever Riker had wanted to use it for.

And when Loch looked over at his best friend again, she smiled and gave him a curious look. Before, he'd tried not to think about the what-ifs, or even look too deeply at what had happened to make him who he was. Yet, with his wife, he couldn't help but do that daily.

She made him a better man. She had always done that.

She left him completely undone, and for that, he'd be forever grateful. Because without her, he wouldn't be who he was. Wouldn't be who his family needed him to be.

"I'd like to propose a toast," Dare said into the noise of family and friends, holding up his glass. The others joined him, and Loch squeezed his wife's hand. "This town, this family has seen it all, done it all. And yet, we're still here." He winked over at Tabby and Alex. "Yeah, some moved to another town, but they're back to visit, and Whiskey will always be a part of their hearts. This town has shaped us all in one way or another, and I'll never be more grateful for what it's brought. So, here's to Whiskey."

"Whiskey is home," Fox added.

"Whiskey is our life," Dare put in.

"Whiskey is family," Loch said, and then the rest added their own replies, but he only had eyes for his wife, his best friend, his everything.

"Love you," he whispered.

She leaned over and kissed his jaw. "Love you more than Whiskey."

And in this town, he knew that meant a whole hell of a lot, because nothing was more important than Whiskey, not in this bootleg town of family, friends, and secrets.

THE END

A Note from Carrie Ann

Thank you so much for reading **WHISKEY UNDONE**. I do hope if you liked this story, that you would please leave a review! Reviews help authors *and* readers.

I hope you loved Loch and Ainsley's romance. I've been waiting forever to write their story so it's about time I got to do it! And I LOVE the fact that it's set in the same world as my Montgomerys so there's always a few surprises for longtime readers!

I know this is the final book in the Whiskey and Lies series, but it's not the end by far for my characters. You might just see them again in the Montgomery Ink world, so keep reading!

Don't miss out on the Montgomery Ink World!

• Montgomery Ink (The Denver Montgomerys)

- Montgomery Ink: Colorado Springs (The Colorado Springs Montgomery Cousins)
- Gallagher Brothers (Jake's Brothers from Ink Enduring)
- Whiskey and Lies (Tabby's Brothers from Ink Exposed)
- Fractured Connections (Mace's Sisters from Fallen Ink)

If you want to make sure you know what's coming next from me, you can sign up for my newsletter at www.Carrie-AnnRyan.com; follow me on twitter at @CarrieAnnRyan, or like my Facebook page. I also have a Facebook Fan Club where we have trivia, chats, and other goodies. You guys are the reason I get to do what I do and I thank you.

Make sure you're signed up for my MAILING LIST so you can know when the next releases are available as well as find giveaways and FREE READS.

Happy Reading!

The Whiskey and Lies Series:
A Montgomery Ink Spin Off Series
Book 1: Whiskey Secrets
Book 2: Whiskey Reveals
Book 3: Whiskey Undone

About Carrie Ann

Carrie Ann Ryan is the New York Times and USA Today

bestselling author of contemporary and paranormal romance. Her works include the Montgomery Ink, Redwood Pack, Talon Pack, and Gallagher Brothers series, which have sold over 2.0 million books worldwide. She started writing while in graduate school for her advanced degree in chemistry and hasn't stopped since. Carrie Ann has written over fifty novels and novellas with more in the works. When she's not writing about bearded tattooed men or alpha wolves that need to find their mates, she's reading as much as she can and exploring the world of baking and gourmet cooking.

www.CarrieAnnRyan.com

More from Carrie Ann

Montgomery Ink: Colorado Springs
Book 1: Fallen Ink
Book 2: Restless Ink
Book 3: Jagged Ink

Montgomery Ink: Boulder
Book 1: Wrapped in Ink

Montgomery Ink:
Book 0.5: Ink Inspired
Book 0.6: Ink Reunited
Book 1: Delicate Ink
Book 1.5: Forever Ink
Book 2: Tempting Boundaries
Book 3: Harder than Words

Book 4: Written in Ink
Book 4.5: Hidden Ink
Book 5: Ink Enduring
Book 6: Ink Exposed
Book 6.5: Adoring Ink
Book 6.6: Love, Honor, & Ink
Book 7: Inked Expressions
Book 7.3: Dropout
Book 7.5: Executive Ink
Book 8: Inked Memories
Book 8.5: Inked Nights
Book 8.7: Second Chance Ink

Fractured Connections
Book 1: Breaking Without You
Book 2: Shouldn't Have You
Book 3: Falling With You

The Whiskey and Lies Series:
Book 1: Whiskey Secrets
Book 2: Whiskey Reveals
Book 3: Whiskey Undone

The Gallagher Brothers Series:
Book 1: Love Restored
Book 2: Passion Restored
Book 3: Hope Restored

The Talon Pack:

Book 1: Tattered Loyalties
Book 2: An Alpha's Choice
Book 3: Mated in Mist
Book 4: Wolf Betrayed
Book 5: Fractured Silence
Book 6: Destiny Disgraced
Book 7: Eternal Mourning
Book 8: Strength Enduring
Book 9: Forever Broken

Redwood Pack Series:
Book 1: An Alpha's Path
Book 2: A Taste for a Mate
Book 3: Trinity Bound
Redwood Pack Box Set (Contains Books 1-3)
Book 3.5: A Night Away
Book 4: Enforcer's Redemption
Book 4.5: Blurred Expectations
Book 4.7: Forgiveness
Book 5: Shattered Emotions
Book 6: Hidden Destiny
Book 6.5: A Beta's Haven
Book 7: Fighting Fate
Book 7.5: Loving the Omega
Book 7.7: The Hunted Heart
Book 8: Wicked Wolf
The Complete Redwood Pack Box Set (Contains Books 1-7.7)

The Branded Pack Series:
(Written with Alexandra Ivy)
Book 1: Stolen and Forgiven
Book 2: Abandoned and Unseen
Book 3: Buried and Shadowed

Dante's Circle Series:
Book 1: Dust of My Wings
Book 2: Her Warriors' Three Wishes
Book 3: An Unlucky Moon
The Dante's Circle Box Set (Contains Books 1-3)
Book 3.5: His Choice
Book 4: Tangled Innocence
Book 5: Fierce Enchantment
Book 6: An Immortal's Song
Book 7: Prowled Darkness
The Complete Dante's Circle Series (Contains Books 1-7)

Holiday, Montana Series:
Book 1: Charmed Spirits
Book 2: Santa's Executive
Book 3: Finding Abigail
The Holiday, Montana Box Set (Contains Books 1-3)
Book 4: Her Lucky Love
Book 5: Dreams of Ivory
The Complete Holiday, Montana Box Set (Contains Books 1-5)

The Happy Ever After Series:

Flame and Ink

Ink Ever After

Single Title:

Finally Found You

Fallen Ink Excerpt

From New York Times Bestselling Author Carrie Ann Ryan's Montgomery Ink: Colorado Springs series

FALLEN INK

Adrienne Montgomery wasn't going to throw up, but it would probably be a close call. It wasn't that she was a nervous person, but today of all days was bound to test her patience and nerves, and she wasn't sure if all those years of growing a spine of steel would be enough.

Maybe she should have worked on forming a steel-lined gut while she was at it—perhaps even a platinum one.

"You're looking pretty pale over there," Mace said, leaning down low to whisper in her ear.

She shivered involuntarily as his breath slid across her neck, and she looked up into her best friend's hazel gaze. The damn man was far too handsome for his own good, and he *knew* she was ticklish, so he constantly spoke in her ear so she shivered like that.

She figured he'd gotten a haircut the day before because the sides were close-cut so you could see the white in his salt-and-pepper hair. He'd let the top grow out, and he had it brushed to the side so it actually looked a little fashionable rather than messy and just hanging in his eyes like most days. Knowing Mace, he'd done it by accident that morning, rather than making it a point to do so. Her best friend was around her age, in his thirties, but had gone salt-and-pepper in his late twenties. While some men might have started dying their hair, Mace had made it work with his ink and piercings—and the ladies liked it.

Well, at least that's what Adrienne figured. It wasn't as if she were one of his following. Not in that way, at least.

"Yo, Adrienne, you okay?"

She glowered, hearing the familiar refrain that had been the bane of her existence since she was in kinder-garten and one of the fathers there had shouted it like the boxer from that movie she now hated.

"What did I say about using that phrase?" She crossed her arms over her chest and tapped her foot. She was at least six inches shorter than her best friend, but since she was wearing her heeled boots, she could at least try to look intimidating.

Mace being Mace just shrugged and winked, giving her that smolder that he'd practiced in the mirror after seeing *Tangled* with her years ago. Yeah, he was *that* guy, the one who liked to make her smile and knew she had a crush on the animated Flynn Rider.

"You know you like it." He wrapped an arm around her shoulder and gave her a tight squeeze. "Now, are you okay? Really? Because you honestly look like you're about to throw up, and with the place all new and shiny, I don't know if vomit really sets the tone."

Thinking about the reason the place—*her* place—was all new and shiny sent her stomach into another roll, and she let out a long breath.

"I'm fine."

Mace just stared at her, and she kicked his shoe. Mature, that was her name. "Try it with a little more enthusiasm, because while I'd *like* to believe you, the panic in your eyes doesn't really portray the right confidence."

"I'll *be* fine. How's that?" she asked and gave him a wide smile. It must have looked a little manic, though, since he winced. But he gave her a thumbs up.

"Okay, then. Let's get out of this office and go out into your brand new tattoo shop to meet the horde."

There went her stomach again.

Her tattoo shop.

She couldn't quite believe it. After years of working for others in Colorado Springs instead of going up north to

Denver to work at her cousins' shop, or even south to New Orleans and her brother's former shop, she was now part-owner of Montgomery Ink Too, the first offshoot of the main shop in downtown Denver.

Yep, she was going to be sick.

"It's mostly family. Not quite a horde." Sort of, at least. Even three people felt like a lot at this point since they'd all be there…waiting for her to say something, do something, *be* someone. And that was enough of that, or she really wouldn't make it out of the office that day.

"True, since most of your family didn't come. The entire Montgomery clan would probably fill four buildings at this point."

"You're not wrong. Only Austin and Maya came down from Denver since Shep and I asked the others to stay home. It would be a little too much for our small building if everyone showed up."

"But your sisters and parents are here, plus Shep and his wife, of course, and I'm pretty sure I saw their baby Livvy out there, too. And then Ryan, since you hired him." Mace stuffed his hands into his pockets. "It's one big, happy family, who happen to be waiting for you to go out there and possibly start a tattoo a bit later for your first client."

After what had seemed like months of paperwork and construction, today was opening day for Montgomery Ink Too—MIT for short. Ryan and Mace had called it that one day, and the nickname had stuck. There was nothing she could do now but go with it, weirdness and all. There had been delays and weather issues, but *finally*, the shop was open. Now, she needed to be an adult and go out into the main room to socialize.

And there went her stomach again.

Mace's strong arms came around her, and she rested her head on his chest, tucking herself under his chin. He had to lift his head a bit so she could fit since she wasn't *that* short, but it was a familiar position for them. No matter what anyone said about Mace, he gave *great* hugs.

"You're going to be fine." His voice rumbled over her, and she could feel the vibrations through his chest and against her cheek.

"You say that now, but what if everything tumbles down and I end up with no clients and ruin the fact that Austin and Maya trusted me with their first satellite shop."

Austin and Maya were two of her numerous Denver cousins. There were eight freaking siblings in that family, and all of them had married off—with Maya having *two* husbands even—so it added up to way too many people for her to count. Maya and Austin owned and operated Montgomery Ink in downtown Denver—what was now the flagship shop it seemed.

Her cousins had come to her over a year ago, saying they were interested in expanding the business. Since real estate was sparse off the 16th Street Mall where Montgomery Ink was located, they'd come up with the idea of opening a new tattoo shop in a different city. And wasn't it nice that they had two other artists in the family so close? Well, Shep hadn't actually been close at the time since he was still living in New Orleans where he'd met his wife and started his family, but now her big brother was back in Colorado Springs and was here to stay.

Maya and Austin were still the main owners of the business and CEOs of the corporation they'd formed in order to add on, but Shep and Adrienne had bought into the franchise and were now partial owners *and* managers of Montgomery Ink Too.

That was a lot of responsibility on her shoulders, but she knew she could do it. She just had to buck up and actually walk into the tattoo shop.

"Stop freaking out, Addi. I wouldn't have come with you on this journey if I didn't believe in you." He pulled away and met her gaze, the intensity so great that she had to blink a few times so she could catch her breath.

He was right. He'd given up a lot for her. Though, in the end, the whole arrangement might work out better for him. Hopefully. He'd left a steady job at their old shop to come and work with her. The trust in that action was staggering, and it gave Adrienne the final bit of strength she needed to do this—whatever *this* was.

"Okay, let's do this."

He held out his hand, and she took it, giving it a squeeze before letting go. It wasn't as if she needed to brace herself against him again or hold his hand as they made their way into the shop. Enough people already wondered just what went on behind closed doors between the two of them. She didn't need to add fuel to the fire.

Mace was just her best friend, nothing more—though certainly nothing less.

He was at her back as she walked through her office door and into the main room, the heat of him keeping her steady. The shop in Colorado Springs matched the one up north in layout, with only a few minor changes. Each station had its own cubicle area, but once people made it past the front section of the shop where onlookers couldn't peep in, it was almost all open. There were two private rooms in the back for those who wanted tattoos that required a little less clothing, as well as folding panels that could be placed in each of the artist's areas so they could be sectioned off easily. Most people didn't mind having other artists and clients watch them while they got a tattoo, and it usually added to the overall experience. As the licensed piercer in residence, Adrienne could do that part of her job in either of the rooms in the back, as well.

While some shops had closed-off rooms for each artist because the building was a converted home or office building, the Montgomerys hadn't wanted that. There was privacy when needed and socialization when desired. It was a great setup, and one Adrienne had been jealous of when she was working at her old place on the other side of the city.

"About time you made your way back here," Maya said dryly, her eyebrow ring glinting under the overhead light.

Adrienne flipped her cousin off then grinned as Maya did the same back. Of all her cousins, she and Maya looked the most alike. They each had long, dark hair, were average height, and had just the right amount of curves to make finding jeans difficult. Of course, Maya had birthed two kids, while Adrienne's butt came from her love of cookies…but that was neither here nor there.

Everyone stood around talking to one another, cups of water or coffee or tea in their hands as they looked around the place. As they weren't opening up for tattoos until later in the day, they were able to easily socialize in the main entry area. Their new hire, Ryan, stood off to the side, and Mace went over to him so they would be out of the way. They were really the only two non-Montgomerys, and she could only imagine how they felt.

"The location is pretty damn perfect," Shep said with a grin. His wife Shea stood by his side, their daughter Livvy bouncing between them. How her niece had gotten so big, Adrienne had no idea. Apparently, time flew when you had your head down, working. "We're the only tattoo shop around here, which will be good for business." They were located in a strip mall off the busiest road in their area—other than I-25, of course. That's how most of the businesses around were set up, with only the large market chains and restaurants having actual acreage behind them.

Adrienne nodded, though her stomach didn't quite agree. Most of the shops like hers were farther south, near the older parts of downtown. There were trendier places there, and a lot more people who looked like they did with ink and piercings. Up north, on North Academy Blvd, every building was the same: cream or tan-colored, and fit in almost like a bedroom community around the Air Force Academy.

Shep and Adrienne wanted not only the cadets but also everyone who lived in the sprawling neighborhood who wanted ink to find them and come back for more. Beginning something new was always difficult, but starting something new in an area of town that, from the outside at least, didn't look as if they'd fit in wouldn't make it any easier.

She knew that a lot of the prejudices about tattoo shops had faded away over time as the art became far more popular and almost normal, but she could still feel people's eyes on her when they noticed her ink.

"It's right next to a tea shop, a deli, a spice shop, Thea's bakery, and a few fancy shopping areas. I think you fit in nicely," Austin said, his arms folded over his chest as he looked around the place. "You almost have a little version of what we have up north. You just need a bookstore and a café where you can hang out."

"You're just spoiled because you don't even have to walk outside into the cold to get coffee or baked goods," Adrienne said dryly.

"That is true," Austin said with a laugh. "Adding in that side door that connects the two businesses was the best decision I ever made."

"I'll be sure to mention that to your wife," Shep said and ducked as Austin's arm shot out. The two men were nearly forty years old but fought like they were teens. Shea picked up Livvy and laughed before heading over to Maya.

Adrienne didn't actually know her sister-in-law all that well since she hadn't seen her much, but now that the family had relocated, she knew that would change.

"They're going to break something," Thea said with a small laugh as she watched the two play-fight. She was the middle girl of the family but tended to act as if she were the eldest. When the retail spot three doors down from Thea's bakery had opened up, her sister had stopped at nothing to make sure Adrienne could move in. That was Thea, taking care of her family no matter what.

"Then they'll deserve it," Roxie, Adrienne's other sister said, shaking her head. "As long as they don't ruin something in the shop, of course," she added quickly after Adrienne shot her a look. "I meant break something on themselves." Roxie was the youngest of their immediate family, and often the quietest. None of them were truly quiet since they were Montgomerys, but Roxie sometimes fit the bill.

"Thanks for thinking of my shop that hasn't even had its first client yet." Adrienne wrapped her arm around Roxie's waist for a hug. "Where's Carter? I thought he said he'd be here."

Roxie and Carter had gotten married a few months ago, and Adrienne loved her brother-in-law, though she didn't know him all that well either. He worked long hours, and the couple tended to be very insular since they were still newlyweds.

Roxie's mouth twisted into a grimace before she schooled her features. "He couldn't get off work. He tried, but two guys called in, and he was up to his neck in carburetors."

Adrienne kissed her sister's temple and squeezed her tightly. "It's okay. It *is* the middle of the day, after all. I'm surprised any of you were able to take time off for this."

Tears formed at the backs of her eyes at the fact that everyone *had* taken the time to be there for her and Shep. She blinked. She looked up from her sisters and tried not to let her emotions get to her, but then she met Mace's eyes. He gave her a curious look, and she smiled at him, trying to let him know that she was okay—just a little overwhelmed. Mace had a way of knowing what she felt without her saying it, and she didn't want him to worry. That's what happened when you were friends with someone as long as they had been.

"I just wish he would have come," Roxie said with a shrug. "It's fine. Everything is fine."

Adrienne met Thea's gaze, but the two sisters didn't say anything. If Roxie had something she wanted to share, she would. For now, everyone had other things on their minds. Namely, opening day.

Shep punched Austin in the shoulder one more time before backing away and grinning. "Okay, okay, I'm too old for this shit."

"True, you *are* too old." Austin winked, and Adrienne pinched the bridge of her nose.

"Great way to show everyone that we're all *so* professional and ready to lead with our own shop," she said, no bite to her tone. This was her family, and she was used to it all. If they weren't joking around and being loveable, adorable dorks, she'd have thought something was wrong.

"It's sort of what we signed on for," Ryan said with a wink. "Right, Mace? I mean, the legendary Montgomery antics are why *any* tattoo artist worth their salt wants to join up with them."

Mace gave them all a solemn nod, laughter dancing in his eyes. "It wouldn't be a Montgomery gathering without someone getting punched. Isn't that what you taught me, Adrienne?"

She flipped him off, knowing that Livvy's head was down so she wouldn't see. She tried not to be *too* bad of an influence on her niece.

"Okay, party people. Finish your drinks and cake and then let's clean up. We have three clients scheduled between one and two this afternoon, and Ryan is handling any walk-ins." Though she wasn't sure there would *be* any walk-ins since it was day one and they were doing a slow start. Some of their long-time clients had moved with them, and they already had a waiting list because of it, but that could change on a dime. Having word of mouth would be what made their shop a success, and that meant getting more clients in who weren't just the same ones from before.

The door opened, and she held back her frown. They weren't officially open yet, but it wasn't as if she could tell a potential customer off. The door *had* been unlocked, after all.

As a man in a nicely cut suit with a frown on his face walked in, Adrienne had a feeling this wouldn't be a client.

"Hi there, can I help you?" she asked, moving her way through the crowd. "We're opening in an hour or so, but if you need any information, I'm here."

The guy's face pinched, and she was worried that if he kept it up, it would freeze like that. "I'm not here for whatever it is this establishment does." His gaze traveled over her family's and friend's ink and clothing before it rested back on her. "I'm only here to tell you that you shouldn't finish unpacking."

"Excuse me?" Shep asked, his tone serious. The others stood back, letting Adrienne and Shep talk, but she knew they were all there if she needed them.

"You heard me." The man adjusted his tie. "I don't know how you got through the zoning board, but I can see they made a mistake. We don't want *your kind* here in our nice city. We're a growing community with families. Like I said, don't unpack. You won't be here long."

Before she could say anything in response to the ridiculous statement, the man turned on his heel and walked out of her building, leaving her family and friends standing beside her, all of them with shocked looks on their faces.

"Well, shit," Mace whispered then winced as he looked behind him to where Livvy was most likely with her mom.

"We'll figure out who that was. But, Adrienne, he won't be able to shut us down or whatever the hell he wants." Shep turned to her and gave her that big-brother stare. "Don't stress about him. He means nothing."

But she could tell from the look in his eyes, and the worried glances passing back and forth between her family members and friends that none of them quite believed that.

She had no idea who the man was, but she had a bad feeling about him. And every single warm feeling that had filled her at the sight of her family and friends coming together to celebrate the new shop fled, replaced by ice water in her veins.

So much for an easy opening day, she thought, and her stomach roiled again. Perhaps she would throw up because she just knew that wasn't the last time they'd see that man. Not by a long shot.

Find out more in FALLEN INK
To make sure you're up to date on all of Carrie Ann's releases, sign up for her mailing list HERE.

Delicate Ink

**From New York Times Bestselling Author Carrie
Ann Ryan's Montgomery Ink Series**

DELICATE INK

On the wrong side of thirty, Austin Montgomery is ready
to settle down. Unfortunately, his inked sleeves and scruffy
beard isn't the suave business appearance some women
crave. Only finding a woman who can deal with his job, as
a tattoo artist and owner of Montgomery Ink, his seven
meddling siblings, and his own gruff attitude won't be easy.

Finding a man is the last thing on Sierra Elder's mind.
A recent transplant to Denver, her focus is on opening her

own boutique. Wanting to cover up scars that run deeper than her flesh, she finds in Austin a man that truly gets to her—in more ways than one.

Although wary, they embark on a slow, tempestuous burn of a relationship. When blasts from both their pasts intrude on their present, however, it will take more than a promise of what could be to keep them together.

Find out more in Delicate Ink. **Out Now.**
To make sure you're up to date on all of Carrie Ann's releases, sign up for her mailing list HERE.

_____

Love Restored
_____

**From New York Times Bestselling Author Carrie
Ann Ryan's Gallagher Brothers series**

Love Restored

In the first of a Montgomery Ink spin-off series from NYT
Bestselling Author Carrie Ann Ryan, a broken man
uncovers the truth of what it means to take a second
chance with the most unexpected woman...

Graham Gallagher has seen it all. And when tragedy
struck, lost it all. He's been the backbone of his brothers,
the one they all rely on in their lives and business. And
when it comes to falling in love and creating a life, he
knows what it's like to have it all and watch it crumble.

He's done with looking for another person to warm his bed, but apparently he didn't learn his lesson because the new piercer at Montgomery Ink tempts him like no other.

Blake Brennen may have been born a trust fund baby, but she's created a whole new life for herself in the world of ink, piercings, and freedom. Only the ties she'd thought she'd cut long ago aren't as severed as she'd believed. When she finds Graham constantly in her path, she knows from first glance that he's the wrong kind of guy for her. Except that Blake excels at making the wrong choice and Graham might be the ultimate temptation for the bad girl she'd thought long buried.

Find out more in Love Restored**. Out Now.**
To make sure you're up to date on all of Carrie Ann's releases, sign up for her mailing list HERE.

CPSIA information can be obtained
at www.ICGtesting.com
Printed in the USA
LVHW051457051118
596010LV00013B/1372/P